TANNER'S TIGER

**Center Point
Large Print**

**This Large Print Book carries the
Seal of Approval of N.A.V.H.**

ॐ श्री गणेशाय नमः

LAWRENCE BLOCK

TANNER'S TIGER

CENTER POINT PUBLISHING
THORNDIKE, MAINE

This Center Point Large Print edition
is published in the year 2002 by arrangement with
Baror International, Inc.

The text of this Large Print edition is unabridged.
In other aspects, this book may vary from the original
edition. Printed in Thailand. Set in 16-point
Times New Roman type by Bill Coskrey.

ISBN 1-58547-172-0

Library of Congress Cataloging-in-Publication Data

Block, Lawrence.
    Tanner's Tiger / Lawrence Block.--Center Point large print ed.
        p. cm.
    ISBN 1-58547-172-0 (lib. bdg. : alk. paper)
    1. Tanner, Evan (Fictitious character)--Fiction. 2. Large type books. I. Title.

PS3552.L63 T37 2002
813'.54--dc21

                                                                2001047766

Our flight left Kennedy at 8:25 on an unusually unpleasant Tuesday night in a generally horrible August. For the past two weeks the people who are supposed to know about such things had been forecasting rain to be followed by a break in the heat. The rain had held off and the heat had prevailed until the weather people appeared to be participants in some sort of meteorological martingale system, resolutely doubling their bets on the *Rain and Cooler* line while *Hot and Clear* turned up day after dismal day. If they didn't hit soon, they would run out of chips. Meanwhile, we were running out of New York.

Not literally running, of course. Flying. Although, after we boarded the big 727 and fastened our seat belts and listened to the little illustrated sermon about proper use of oxygen masks, it appeared as though we were neither running nor flying from New York to Montreal. Instead, it looked as if we were going to drive there.

The plane taxied to and fro, to and fro. The pilot put many miles on the aircraft without yet leaving the ground. Minna squeezed my hand. I looked down at her and she pouted up at me.

"You promised we would fly," she said.

"We will. Be patient."

"Is this really an airplane?"

"Of course."

"It does not behave like one."

Minna had flown once before, on a Russian experimental jet fighter-bomber that we had hijacked from a missile base in Estonia. That time we had taken off vertically, and I could understand how our little promenade on the runway might be a letdown for her. I assured her that the 727 was really a plane and that it would soon behave in a planelike manner. I don't think she believed me.

After another fifteen minutes of driving, the pilot introduced himself apologetically over the intercom. I thought he was going to tell us that there was a bomb on the plane or that Montreal had been closed for the season. He explained, anticlimactically, I thought, that there were still six planes ahead of us, that we would get assigned to a runway sooner or later, and that he thanked us for our patience.

Minna said something unforgivable in Lithuanian.

"Watch it," I said.

"But no one can understand me, Evan."

"That's the point." I patted her little hand. "Don't speak anything but English until we get into Canada. Remember, you're an American citizen, you were born in New York, your name is Minna Tanner, and you speak only English."

"All right. The pilot is a—"

"Proper English."

"—nice man."

She is not an American citizen, she was not born in New York, her name is not Minna Tanner, and I'm not entirely certain how many languages she speaks. She is fluent in Lithuanian, Lettish, English, and Puerto Rican Spanish, and has accumulated bits and pieces of many other languages from the books and records and occasional guests in my apartment, where I live and she reigns. She is the sole surviving descendant of Mindaugas, who in his turn was the sole king of independent Lithuania some seven centuries ago.

When I first met her, she was living in a cheerless basement room in the Lithuanian Soviet Socialist Republic, tended by a pair of addled old maids who awaited the day when she could be installed as Lithuania's queen. I took her away from all that, and now she plays queen in my somewhat less cheerless apartment on West 107th Street. From time to time I threaten to send her to school or to have her adopted by some happy little couple with a happy little house out in a happy little suburb. She and I both know that this will never happen—she's too much fun to have around. Ever since Kitty Bazerian's grandmother taught her how to make Armenian coffee, she has become utterly indispensable.

"How long will we be on this plane, Evan?"

"The flight takes an hour. If we ever get off the ground."

"And then we will be in Montreal?"

"Yes. And our luggage will be in Buenos Aires."

"Buenos Aires?"

"I never trust airlines. I'm joking. We'll be in Montreal when the plane lands, yes."

"Can we go to Expo tonight?"

"It'll be too late."

"I'm not tired, Evan."

"You'll be tired by the time we get to the hotel."

"I won't. I'm hardly ever tired, Evan. Like you, I need very little sleep. Hardly any sleep at all."

I looked at her. Minna averages ten hours of sleep in twenty-four, which is a fairly healthy average. I sleep not at all, having lost the habit forever when a shard of North Korean shrapnel performed random brain surgery and

7

knocked out something called the sleep center. I have been awake ever since. My disability pay is $112 per month, and I don't have to spend a cent of it on pajamas.

"If we went to Expo tonight," Minna said carefully, "I could sleep late tomorrow. I wouldn't want you to have to postpone your visit to Expo just because of me. I would be willing to stay up late tonight and sleep tomorrow."

"That's very thoughtful of you."

"It's nothing."

"Last Saturday you were equally selfless. You volunteered to accompany Sonya to the children's zoo."

"She wanted to see it, Evan. And adults are not permitted unless they are accompanied by children. I thought to do her a favor."

She has worked the children's zoo con on every woman I've ever brought to the apartment. "If you want," I said, "we'll go to Expo tonight."

"I only wish to be fair with you. Oh, I think it is an airplane after all!"

And so it was. We had clearance at last, and the big jet roared down the runway and took off. I sat back in my seat while Minna pressed her face to the window, watching the ground fall away from us.

Once it was off the ground, the plane behaved superbly. I had a drink and Minna had a glass of milk, and by the time we were finished the pilot was once again on the intercom, mumbling something about fastening our seat belts for the descent to Duval Airport. Since we hadn't unfastened them, this was no problem. The landing was smooth. The plane taxied to a stop and we left it.

We followed the crowd into the airport and queued up for

the luggage. The bags came spilling down a ramp onto a circular baggage rack that rotated. I missed our suitcase the first time around and waited until it made its way to us a second time. We got into another line that led past a desk where an attendant with a French accent sent Canadians to the left and Americans to the right. We went to the right. There were three lines, and we picked the shortest one.

I had our passports in my jacket pocket. You do not need a passport to get into Canada or back into the States, but the airlines clerk had recommended carrying proof of citizenship, and anyway I like to have my passport with me when I travel.

My passport was a forgery, but it had passed muster so many times I was no longer nervous about it. A gentle old Armenian man had made it for me some time ago in Athens, after the Czech government had confiscated my real passport. The forgery had all the proper information on it, including the original passport number, so I wasn't worried about it. Minna's passport, on the other hand, was genuine government issue. All we had needed to obtain it was a New York City birth certificate, and a Croat Nationalist on Norfolk Street had made that up for me in fifteen minutes, no charge. I had done him a favor once.

"Your name is Minna Tanner, you were born in New York City," I said.

"I know, I know."

"I'm your father."

"I know."

The line moved onward and we came to the front of it. The customs attendant had wavy black hair and a thin nose. He smiled and asked us our names.

"Evan Michael Tanner," I said.

"Minna Tanner," Minna said.

"You are United States citizens?"

"Yes."

"Yes."

"You were born?"

"Yes," said Minna.

I winced. He smiled. "*Where* were you born?" he asked gently.

"New York City."

"New York City."

"Yes," he said. "And why have you come to Montreal, Mr. . . ."

"Tanner. To see the fair."

"To see the fair. You will stay how long?"

"About a week."

"About a week. Yes." He started to say something, and then he stopped and frowned for a moment, and then he looked at me as if seeing me for the first time. "Evan Tanner, Evan Tanner," he said. "I am sorry, Mr. Tanner, but you have perhaps some identification?"

His French accent was thicker now. I handed him our passports. He examined them, studied my photo and Minna's, studied my face and Minna's, went over the passports again, whistled soundlessly, and got to his feet. "You will excuse me for one moment, please," he said, and went away.

Minna looked at me. "Something is wrong?"

"Evidently."

"What?"

"I don't know."

10

"Something is wrong with the passports?"

"I can't imagine what."

"You said that it was very simple to go into Canada. That it was hardly like going from one country to another."

"I know."

"I do not understand."

"Neither do I."

"Where did the man go?"

I shrugged. Perhaps, I thought, they had received a circular on some criminal with a similar name. Perhaps some clown named Ivan Manners had embezzled a few hundred thousand dollars from the Keokuk National Bank. I couldn't imagine what else could stop him cold like that.

He came back, finally, following an older man with gray hair and a small mustache. The older man said "Come with me, please," just as the younger one was saying, "You will please go with him." We did. The gray-haired man led us down a corridor to a small room with an armed guard in front of it. Minna held my hand and did not utter a sound.

There was only one chair, a rather severe wooden affair behind the desk. The gray-haired man sat in it and we stood in front of the desk and looked over it at him. He had our passports in front of him, along with a batch of papers that he shuffled through.

"I don't understand this," I said. "What's the problem?"

"Evan Tanner," he said.

"Yes."

"Evan Michael Tanner of New York City."

"Yes, I don't—"

He narrowed his eyes at me. "Perhaps you might tell me, Mr. Tanner, just why you are so intent upon separating the

Province of Québec from the Dominion of Canada?"

"Oh."

"Indeed." He played again with the pile of papers. "You are not Canadian," he said. "Nor are you French. You have never lived in Québec. You have no family here. Yet you are a member, as I understand it, of the most radical of the separatist organizations, Le Mouvement National de Québec. Why?"

"Because differences in language and culture constitute differences in nationality," I heard myself say. "Because Québec has always been French and will always be French, Wolfe's victory over Montcalm notwithstanding. Because two centuries of British colonialism cannot change the basic fact that French Canada and British Canada have nothing in common. Because a house divided against itself cannot stand. Because—"

"Please, Mr. Tanner." He put his hand to his forehead. "Please . . ."

I had not meant to say all that. I hadn't meant to say any of it, really. It just sort of happened.

"I do not require statements of political philosophy from you, Mr. Tanner. One can hear all the extremist nonsense one wishes these days. One can read yards of that lunacy in the separatist press. I have heard all these arguments and know them to be fundamentally absurd. It is even difficult for me to believe that native French Canadians can swallow such a tissue of lies, but apparently a tiny percentage of them can and does. Every society has its lunatic fringe." He shook his head, deploring the existence of lunatics and fringes. "But you are neither French nor Canadian. I repeat—what is your interest? Why do you intrude in affairs that concern you not at all?"

"I sympathize with the cause."

"A cause that is not your own?"

It was pointless to argue with him. One either identifies with little ragged bands of political extremists or considers them to be madmen; one either embraces lost causes or deplores them. I could have told this odious man that I was also a member of the League for the Restoration of Cilician Armenia, the Pan-Hellenic Friendship Society, the Irish Republican Brotherhood, the Internal Macedonian Revolutionary Organization, the Flat Earth Society—I could have gone on at great length, but why alienate him any further? It would have been a lost cause, and I was already committed to enough of those.

"Why have you come to Montreal, Mr. Tanner?"

"To see Expo."

"Of course you do not expect me to believe that."

"I guess not."

"Would you care to tell me the truth?"

"I already have, but you're right, I don't expect you to believe it."

He pushed his chair back and got to his feet. He turned away from us and walked to the far wall, his hands clasped behind his back. I looked at Minna. She did not look at all happy.

"Mr. Tanner?"

"Yes?"

"You plan demonstrations in Montreal? Another outburst of terrorism?"

"I planned to see the fair. That's all."

"The Queen is honoring us with a visit, you know. Is

your own visit somehow connected with hers?"

"I don't even know the woman."

His hands formed fists. He closed his eyes and went rigid all over. For a happy moment I thought he was going to have a stroke. Then he calmed himself down and found his way back into his chair. "I will not waste time with you," he said. "The MNQ is a joke, a minor irritation. It is not worth our attention. It was foolish of you to attempt to enter Canada and disgusting that you would bring a child with you on such a mission. Of course you must return directly to the United States, you are *persona non grata* here. I will thank you to concern yourself with American affairs and leave Canadian matters to Canadians." He consulted a piece of paper. "There is a flight to New York leaving in an hour and twenty minutes. You and your daughter will be on it. You will not return to Canada. Do you understand?"

Minna said, "We can not go to Expo, Evan?"

"That's what the man says."

The man leaned over his desk to smile at Minna. The world's worst scoundrels always attempt to display their humanity by smiling at children. "I would like to take you to see the fair, little girl, but your father is not allowed in our country."

"Your mother," said Minna in Armenian, "is a flea-ridden harlot who has unpardonable relations with the beasts of the field."

He looked at me. "What language is that?"

"French," I said.

They kept us in that room until our flight was boarding, and when Minna had to go to the ladies' room, they sent a matron along with her. They gave me our passports as they put us on the plane, and this time there was no long wait for runway clearance. The flight back to New York was as pleasantly dull as the flight to Montreal. I had two drinks this time, and Minna had another glass of milk, and then we landed at Kennedy. It was close to one o'clock in the morning, Minna was asleep on her feet, and I was ready to dynamite the Canadian Embassy.

I have traveled illegally through most of the world. I have crossed international frontiers on foot, in donkey carts, in automobile trunks, almost every way imaginable. I've border-hopped through the Balkans and the Soviet Union. I drove a Russian tank across the demilitarized zone from North to South Vietnam.

And I couldn't get into Canada.

2

Canada.
  I hadn't even wanted to go there in the first place. I had nothing against the country and had enjoyed myself the few times I'd been in Montreal, but the world was full of places I would just as soon be. The Expo was supposed to be a grand thing for Canada, and I was glad it was there; I'm glad the sun's up there in the sky, but that doesn't make me anxious to visit it. I had attended the last World's Fair, in New York. I spent a day standing in various lines and came home with the conviction that the world could have all the fairs it wanted but that it would have to have them without me.

Minna mentioned Expo a couple of times in approximately the tone of voice she used when discussing the Central Park Zoo. I made it obvious to her that we weren't going, and she gave up. The summer began shaping up nicely. There was a Ukrainian girl named Sonya who was spending a lot of time around the apartment. There was the usual heavy volume of mail to contend with six days a week. There were books and pamphlets and magazines to read, a set of Bantu language records to master, meetings and discussion groups to attend, and, on the business side, a thesis to be written. It was hot as hell outside, but I had an air-conditioner in the apartment and they said the heat would break any day.

Then things began to go to hell.

The first thing to go was the air-conditioner. The heat, as I have mentioned, got worse instead of better, and the forecasters kept being wrong, and the air-conditioner just couldn't keep up with it all. It dropped dead. It took me two days to get a repairman to look at it, and he collected ten dollars for a house call and took only ten minutes to assure me that the machine was not repairable.

It was an old unit, so that much was only irritating. What was aggravating was the impossibility of replacing the damned thing. The middle of a heat wave is not the best time to order an air-conditioner. The best time, I guess, is in early February, when no one else has the same idea. I called all over town until my fingers had blisters from walking through the Yellow Pages. The best promise I could get was three weeks' delivery time.

After the air-conditioner died, Sonya moved out, though whether or not there was a direct cause-and-effect relationship, I cannot say. With the thermometer hovering between ninety-five and a hundred, the physical benefits of her companionship were beyond the pale anyway, but it was most unfortunate that our relationship terminated as it did. She put too much chervil in the scrambled eggs, and I was less than diplomatic in calling this fact to her attention. We started shouting at each other. Under more normal circumstances we would have kissed and made up, but the heat made that impossible. It was easier to fight. She threw the scrambled eggs at me, and then she went to the refrigerator and gathered up the other eggs, the raw and as yet unscrambled ones, and began throwing those here and there. One of them wound up in the record player, and I didn't discover it until the next day when it cooked there while I played a Bantu language record.

Outside, the city was going to screaming hell around me. There was a three-day riot in Brooklyn, in the Bedford-Stuyvesant section. Some broker ran amok on his lunch hour and shot up Wall Street with an air pistol. Some cops had beaten up some hippies in Tompkins Square Park. The cab drivers were threatening a strike. The social workers were threatening a strike. The garbagemen were threatening a strike.

I drank a lot of iced tea and tried to concentrate on the thesis I was writing, a doctoral bit on the implications of the Methuen Treaty upon the War of the Spanish Succession. It was a particularly interesting theme and I was having a lot of fun with the research, and when I was about three-fourths of the way through it, Roger Carmody called up and told me I might as well forget it because he had failed his oral examinations and had decided to say the hell with it and join the Army.

I had put a price of $1750 on the thesis, which was reasonable enough. And I had collected half the money in advance, mine to keep now that the job was washed out, but Roger Carmody was a pretty nice fellow and I felt bad about the whole deal, so I gave him all his money back and consequently felt even worse about the whole deal. Someday I would finish the thesis for somebody else and get my money out of it. In the meanwhile my bank balance was lower than I like to have it.

It was just one damned thing after another. A batch of things was hanging in the air in an annoying fashion. In Macedonia a girl named Annalya, the mother of my son Todor, was expecting a second child momentarily; I couldn't find out a thing about her, and some friends of mine who were normally in close contact with Macedonia didn't know anything. Other good friends had gone over to Africa to assist a secessionist movement in one of the new states and had quietly disappeared from the face of the earth. No one had any idea what had happened to them, and as they had been last seen in cannibal territory, it was quite probable that they had been eaten.

Then I got an eviction notice from my idiot landlord.

It turned out to be a mistake, of course. My landlord had hired a new secretary, and either she was particularly stupid or he had been singularly incompetent in drilling her in standard procedures, because she had sent eviction notices to every tenant in the half dozen buildings he owned. In my case, all that transpired was an apoplectic phone call, but with a great many of his other tenants he wasn't so lucky. They *were* behind in their rent, and were used to things like eviction notices, so they moved. Just like that, the poor clown had a third of his apartments vacant and not a chance of collecting all the back rent.

I suppose he fired the girl. I suppose she went home and yelled at her mother or threw a shoe at the cat. I suppose the cat ran off and scratched someone. It was that kind of summer, and each day was worse than the last one.

By then I knew that the heat wave wasn't going to end. I didn't care what the weather bureau said, it was going to remain hot until I got a new air-conditioner. I was positive of it. Everything was going wrong; all of civilization was gradually crumbling around me. I sat in my apartment and read the Book of Jeremiah and waited for the world to end.

And then, of course, I got a message from the Chief.

I'll have to explain about the Chief. I don't know very much about him, but then neither does anyone else. He heads some sort of ultrasecret government agency. I don't know its name, nor, for that matter, do I know the Chief's name. As far as I can tell, his outfit handles the sort of operations that call for individual agents left on their own initiative and operating from deep cover. While the Central Intelligence Agency, for example, uses elaborate courier nets, the Chief's men don't even know each other. They don't file formal reports, are forbidden even to get in touch with their own headquarters, and are generally left to work things out on their own.

The Chief thinks I'm one of his men.

Maybe I am. It's hard to say. He once sprang me from a CIA dungeon somewhere in darkest Washington and since then he has made contact from time to time to hand me assignments. I'd rather he wouldn't do this, but the man is convinced I'm one of his most reliable operatives, and I've never been able to figure out a way to change his mind. Besides, there's something to be said for the connection—as it stands. I'm under fairly constant surveillance by the CIA, which is sure I am some kind of secret agent, never mind whose, and by the FBI, which is positive I am six different kinds of subversive. With all of the consequent wiretapping and mail-snooping going on, it's vaguely reassuring to have at least one government factotum who thinks, right or wrong, that I'm on his side.

The message from the Chief came in my morning mail the Thursday before Minna and I flew to Montreal. I suppose he figured that once the FBI censors had read my mail, anything that got into my mailbox was safe from them. Anyway, when I hauled the mail up to my room, there was one envelope with just my name on it, no address, no stamp, no return address, nothing. In the envelope was a matchbook from something called Hector's Lounge, in Helena, Montana. I checked to see if anyone had written anything anywhere. No one had.

I knew it had to be him. None of the marginal subversives in any of the groups I belonged to would ever think of anything quite so cute. I turned the matchbook over and over in my hands. It was trying to tell me something, but it had been struck mute.

I left the building and walked through the heat to a drugstore on Broadway. In the phone booth I dialed the area code for Helena, Montana, which, if you care, is 406. Then I dialed the seven digits for Hector's Lounge. It rang a few times, and then an operator cut in and asked me what number I was calling, please, and I learned that the number I was calling did not exist, and neither did Hector's Lounge.

I had a Coke at the counter. If someone ever wished me ill, I thought, all he really had to do was gimmick me to death. He could keep leaving cryptic messages for me, all of them quite meaningless, and I would run myself ragged calling nonexistent telephone numbers and otherwise making an ass of myself. Maybe one was supposed to immerse the matchbook in water. I asked the counterman for a glass of water, and immersed the matchbook in it, and tried not to notice the way he was staring at me. All that happened was that the matchbook got predictably soggy, and some of the red gunk at the tips of the matches came off.

I went back to the phone, dialed 202 for Washington, and then the number again. I got somebody in the Bureau of Health, Education, and Welfare. He didn't know just what I wanted and I didn't know just who he was, and I wasted my time and his until I established that Hector's Lounge meant nothing to him.

I looked in the phone book under Hector's Lounge and found out that there was such a place right in Manhattan, on Sixth Avenue in the Forties. The listed number was not the same as the one on the matchbook. I dialed it and nobody answered the phone.

Then I dialed the number from the matchbook, without bothering with area codes, and that turned out to be what the Chief had had in mind. Maybe I should have done it that way in the first place, I don't know. Maybe that's what everyone else would have done. Make things sufficiently complicated and almost anybody can find a way to foul them up.

I dialed the number, and a woman answered it in the middle of the first ring. She said, "Yes?"

I asked if this was Hector's Lounge.

"It is," she said.

"May I speak with Hector?"

"Who's calling, please?"

"Helena," I said.

She gave me an address, a second-floor loft on Gansevoort Street in the bowels of the West Village. I took the IRT subway to Sheridan Square and groped around until I found the place. The loft smelled of untanned leather, and hides were stacked in bales all over the place. It was infernally hot in there. A noisy old fan on a tripod blew warm air at me.

My other meetings with him have always taken place in comfortable rooms or suites in good hotels. Now, on a day like this one, he had picked one of the few places in New York (aside from my damned apartment) that was not air-conditioned. He sat in a leather chair, then got to his feet at my approach and crossed the areaway to shake hands. He had already sweated through his shiny gray suit, and he looked as uncomfortable as he had every right to be. "Ah, Tanner," he said. "Excuse this heat and this mess."

He sat down. His was the only chair in the room. He nodded vaguely at a bundle of hides and I sat on it. He picked up a bottle and a couple of glasses.

"Scotch?"

"With a lot of ice."

"I'm afraid there's no ice," he said.

We drank our drinks and chatted. I asked him if he happened to know anything about the friends of mine who were lost in Africa, and he said that as far as he knew, they had been eaten. I had already come to that conclusion myself, but it would have been nice to know something more definite, one way or the other. One can resign oneself to a loss, even in such barbaric circumstances, but it's dreary to have the whole business up in the air. Better the horrible fact than the probability.

"Cuba," the Chief said suddenly. "Keep in touch with Cuba, Tanner?"

"Slightly."

"Refugee groups, that sort of thing?"

"Yes." Half of Florida belongs to one Cuban refugee group or another, and I know people in most of them. My favorite is the band that runs gunboats in the Caribbean sinking ships en route to Havana. Fidel doesn't pay too much attention to them, but the U.S. government makes their life rather difficult, and I think they can use all the support they can get. "Yes," I said, "I know some men involved in those groups."

"Thought you might. You were also involved in one of the front organizations, weren't you? Play Fair with Fidel or something?"

"Fair Play for Cuba."

"That's the one."

"It wasn't exactly a front organization," I said. "The Cuban government supported it, of course, but it was more than a straight propaganda outlet at the time. Leftist-dominated, naturally. An organization composed of people who were concerned that the United States might interfere in the internal affairs of Cuba."

"Mmmm."

"An unwarranted assumption, of course. The Bay of Pigs showed as much."

"It did?" He looked at me oddly, seemed about to say something, then sighed shortly and lifted the Scotch bottle. I was perspiring far too heavily to want anything without ice, especially whiskey. He helped himself to another small drink and tossed it off.

"Where were we?"

"Cuba."

"Yes. Not our normal bailiwick, you know. The Boy Scouts generally keep an eye on that part of the hemisphere."

"Still?"

"Yes, even now. To err is human, that seems to be the official line. And naturally they want to stay with it, you know. I think they hope to improve their track record down there."

"Shouldn't be hard."

"Not at all." He put down his glass, placed his pudgy hands in his lap, and folded them. I waited for him to tell me that I had to go to Havana, disguised as a worker in the canefields, to shave Fidel in his sleep. Havana would be just the place in August. It was the only city I could think of offhand that was almost certain to be warmer than New York. It was bad enough to be handed an assignment that was dangerous, stupid, and immoral. This one promised to be all of those, and uncomfortable in the bargain.

"I may be sending you on a wild-goose chase, Tanner."

"Oh."

"I almost handed the whole thing back myself when I

first got wind of it. Almost told them to give it to the Boy Scouts. They've got the manpower to spare, they can afford to send people on fool's errands, and a lot of their personnel aren't geared for much better than that. Almost gave it back, Tanner, but then I thought of you."

I did not say any of the things that occurred to me.

"Felt you might be right for it. If there's anything to it, that is. If there's any game at all, not to speak of whether or not it's worth the candle. But your background, your contacts, your languages, your special talents—I thought it might be down your alley."

"I see," I lied.

"You can turn it down if you want."

"It's like that?"

"Yes." He sighed, started to lift the Scotch bottle, then set it down again. I've never seen him drunk and I don't believe I've ever seen him not drinking. Perhaps he's drunk all the time and it simply doesn't show. I drew a deep breath and began to think of reasons why I couldn't possibly go to Havana. My mind wasn't working well. I think it was the overwhelming smell of leather that was getting to me. I had always liked the smell of leather before.

"I would like you to go—"

"To Havana," I said.

"Havana?" He looked confused. "No, not Havana. Why on earth should you go to Havana? I want you to go to Montreal."

"It's the Cuban Pavilion," he was saying. "You know there's a World's Fair in Montreal this year. Expo, they call it. Man and His World, that's the theme of it. Makes things rather simple for the exhibitors, wouldn't you say? I'd be hard put to think of anything that wouldn't fit the overall theme of Man and His World. Even Sally Rand, for heaven's sake.

"Cuba is one of the participating nations. The theme of the Cuban Pavilion is revolution. Or Man and His Revolution, I don't know. Quite a shocking display they have, from what I hear. All the other countries offer rather pleasant displays of native crafts and burgeoning industry and dynamic agriculture, and the Cubans confront one with posters and machine guns and the most blatant propaganda in history. One walks past all of these screaming posters, then enters their little restaurants and has a rum drink and a Havana cigar. That's what they're selling—rum and cigars and revolution."

"Is it successful propaganda?"

"Probably not. I suspect that family groups parade through, then say something like, 'That was nice, now let's ride on the Minirail.' It's hard to measure the effect of such intangibles."

I was sort of lost. I was still trying to get used to the idea that he was sending me, not to Havana, but to Montreal. Montreal, I kept thinking, was 400 miles *north* of New York. North. It was almost certain to be cooler in Montreal. And Minna had been badgering me to take her there anyway. And there wouldn't be any race riots there, or any cab strikes or social worker strikes, and my landlord wouldn't be there, and—

"I'm not sure I understand," I said. "You don't want me to blow up the Cuban Pavilion—"

"Heavens, no!"

"Or organize demonstrations around it, or anything?"

"No."

"Then what? I mean, Havana spends three-quarters of its time launching anti-American propaganda of one sort or another. This seems like one of their less effective ways to do it, since ninety-five percent of the people exposed to it will be Americans or Canadians. I don't—"

"No one's worried about the propaganda aspect, Tanner."

"What is it, then?"

He closed his eyes for a moment. He opened them and said, "I wish to hell I knew." He cleared his throat. "I keep losing track of things today. It's this damned heat. It's nearly as bad as Washington."

"It's this bad in Washington?"

"Worse, far worse." He cleared his throat again. "The Cuban Pavilion. We've been receiving strange reports about their whole operation there. They seem to be using the pavilion as a base for some sort of secret operation. One story has it that they're using it as an infiltration point for agents who then make their way into the States masquerading as American tourists. Another report suggests that they plan a big push in U.S. Negro and Puerto Rican neighborhoods, some sort of involvement in the riots. It sounds farfetched, doesn't it? But they've blamed the damned riots on everyone else lately, I suppose they ought to charge Fidel with them. The point is this—any single one of these rumbles we've received would be worth permanent filing in the wastepaper basket. As it stands, though, we're receiving too much static. We can't discount all of it. The Cubans are doing something improper with that pavilion, and we don't know what the hell it is, and we feel we ought to know." He closed his eyes again. "Am I making sense to you?"

"Yes."

"I ask because I myself find it hard to take all of this as seriously as it probably in fact deserves to be taken. You see what the assignment boils down to, Tanner? I'd like you to take a look at the Cuban Pavilion. Stick your nose in, spend a bit of time there, try to get an idea what the hell is going on. Perhaps you can sort of worm your way in, develop some sort of contact with their employees. You speak Spanish—"

"That can't be much help."

"Won't hurt. Your political background might be worthwhile. You might be able to . . . oh, I don't want to tell you your job, Lord knows you're a professional at this sort of thing. If anyone can sort the fact from the fiction, you can. But at the same time, I hate to have you waste your time in what might well be nothing for us at all. Have you got anything of your own on the fire? Anything really promising?"

What a marvelous opportunity to duck an assignment! He was very nearly begging me to cop out.

"Nothing at the moment."

"Anything that could pop soon?"

"Not really."

"Hmmmm. Would you like to give it a shot, then?"

Did I care what was happening at the Cuban Pavilion? No. Did I want to see the fair? No. Did I want to go to Montreal? No. Did I want to get out of New York?

"Yes," I said.

He insisted on advancing me money for plane fare, chuck-

28

ling as he pointed out that I never seemed to turn in expense requests after a trip. I told him that I usually managed to make expenses on assignments, and he chuckled again and muttered something about resourceful operatives and individual initiative. "But I can't think you'll find any personal profit in this trip, Tanner. After all, you're only going to Canada."

I told him that I thought I would take my little girl along. He said she would make a good cover, and advanced money for her ticket as well. I hadn't thought of Minna as part of a cover, somehow. I just thought she'd like to see the damned fair and that it wouldn't hurt her to get out of the oven that called itself New York.

I left him there with the leather. On 42nd Street I picked up tickets on the first available flight to Montreal, which was Tuesday night. Everything before then was booked solid. The clerk told me to take proof of citizenship. I already had Minna's passport, having applied for it long before there was any specific place I wanted to take her. Anyone who doesn't possess a passport in good order is a fool. No man is so secure that the possibility does not exist that someday he will find it necessary to go someplace far away in a hurry.

I took a cab back to my apartment. An air-conditioned cab. I hated to leave it. I climbed four flights of stairs. Warm air rises—the higher I climbed, the warmer it was. I let myself into my place and found Minna listening to the radio and reading a copy of the general orders of the Latvian Army-In-Exile. "Better brush up your French," I said. "Tuesday night we leave for Montreal."

"Montreal!"

"Unless you don't want to—"

"Oh, Evan! You're taking me to Expo?"

"I'm taking you to Expo."

But now it looked as though I weren't.

3

At Kennedy I carried Minna from the plane. One of my fellow passengers made cute faces at her; Minna, being asleep, fortunately missed them. "She's a cutie," he said. "Out cold, isn't she?"

"So it seems."

"Must have had a wonderful time at Expo. The kids all have a ball. You should have seen mine. Stay long?"

"Not very long," I said.

Minna came awake while I waited for our suitcase. She wanted to know where we were and I told her we were in New York. For a few moments she fell silent. Then she asked, for the first time, why we had not been allowed to go to the fair. Because those men were stupid, I told her, and wouldn't let us into their country.

"Did we do something bad?"

"No."

"Is it because I am not really your daughter?"

"No. It's because I'm me."

"I don't understand."

"It doesn't matter." I hefted the suitcase, which seemed to have gained weight in transit. "You must be exhausted."

"What time is it?"

"Almost one."

"The Expo is closed for the night now."

"Probably."

She thought this over. "Where are we going now?"

"Where would you like to go?"

"The toilet."

I waited for her outside the ladies' room. She reappeared with a thoughtful expression on her face. "I suppose we ought to go home," she said.

"No."

"No?"

"We're going to Canada."

"But they won't let us."

"Well, the hell with them," I said. "We'll find a motel near here and . . . Minna, do you think you could sleep on an airplane?"

"I am not sleepy."

"Uh-huh. Sure." I steered her to a chair and told her to wait for me, then found my way to the American Airlines ticket counter. There I learned that we had just missed the last flight to Buffalo, that the first morning flight would leave at 4:55. I got us a pair of one-way tickets on it, checked our suitcase, and went back to Minna. She was sound asleep. She went on sleeping while I drank coffee and read the *Times*. When they ultimately called our flight, I carried her onto the plane, and she didn't open her eyes until takeoff, when she sat bolt upright and began talking senselessly in Lithuanian, some gibberish about horses and pigs. I asked her what she was talking about and she closed her eyes and fell back asleep. She awoke again in the Buffalo airport. The sun was up, the early morning air already thick and humid.

The airlines still hadn't lost our suitcase. I rescued it, and we had breakfast there at the airport and killed time until it was late enough to call people. I took a batch of dimes to the phone booth and started dialing. Two of the people I tried had moved, and four more were already at work, and I was beginning to run out of contacts. I looked up one of my less hopeful prospects in the telephone book and dialed his number, and the man who answered sounded as though he had been drunk for at least eight months.

I said, "Mr. Pryzeshweski?"

"Yeah."

"Mr. Jerzy Pryzeshweski?"

"Yeah, thiz Jerry. Whozit?"

I said, "Mr. Pryzeshweski, my name is Evan Tanner. I don't believe we've ever met, but I'm a very good friend of—"

He said, "See ya, friend," and hung up.

I looked at the phone for a few seconds, then invested another dime and called him again. This time he sounded a little more awake. He told me I was a goddamned sonofabitch and he had to get some sleep.

So I said, in Polish, "Jerzy, comrade, my good friend Taddeusz Orlowicz told me to call you if ever I needed assistance in Buffalo. I am on vital business for the movement, Jerzy, and I am calling you because—"

"Jeez, you a Polack?"

"Yes, I—"

"You know Tad?"

"He is my good friend. I—"

"Well, what do you know!" He laughed loudly into the phone and I pulled it away from my ear. "How is the old drunk broadchaser? I'll be a son of a bitch, Tad Orlowicz.

I thought he was dead."

"He's not. He—"

"I didn't see Tad since, oh, I don't know how long. He went back to the old country, huh?"

"I saw him last year in Cracow."

"No kidding. Still drinking the booze, huh? Still chasing the girls?"

I closed my eyes. "Same as ever," I said.

"Same old Tad!"

"Same old Tad."

"Well, what do you know. Wha'd you say your name was?"

"Tanner," I said, "Evan Tanner."

"Well, what's it all about, huh?"

"I have to see you. I can't talk on the phone."

"No kidding?"

I closed my eyes again. There were, I thought, over a hundred thousand Poles in the city of Buffalo, still more in the surrounding suburbs. With such a large subculture to draw from, it was inconceivable that the Society for a Free Poland didn't have a more efficient operative in the area. SFP had dozens of activists in and around Buffalo, but the others whose names I was able to remember had not been home.

I thought of hanging up and trying to find someone else or simply going ahead under my own steam. I couldn't avoid the feeling that Jerzy Pryzeshweski would bungle any task assigned to him.

Still, though, he did seem to know Taddeusz, who was as fond of women and vodka as Jerzy said he was, and who combined a true patriot's zeal for Polish freedom with

33

irreverent contempt for the Polish people. Taddeusz had saved me from arrest and execution in Cracow and sent me on my way to Lithuania; maybe his chum Jerzy could handle the less burdensome chore of smuggling me into Canada.

So what I said was, "I need your help. Can I come to your home?"

"You in town?"

"Yes."

"Sure, come by my house. You know how to get here? Where are you, the bus? You got a car?"

"I'll be right over," I said.

He lived in a little ranch house in a neat little suburb called Cheektowaga. It was not far from the airport and the cab-driver found it easily. Jerzy was sitting on the front porch when we got there. He was wearing a pair of heavy brown shoes, khaki trousers, and a shiny yellow-green shirt that said *Bowl-a-Lot Lanes* on the back, *Kleinman's Bakery Products* on the front, and *Jerry Press* on the pocket. He was sitting in an aluminum frame chair with green and yellow webbing, and he was drinking a can of beer, and he weighed close to three hundred pounds.

"You should of told me, I would of come for you," he said. "Why waste money on a cab? Listen, you want a beer?"

"Sure."

"How about the kid?"

Minna said beer was fine, and I said it wasn't and asked if he had any milk, and he didn't. We settled on a Coke. Jerzy Pryzeshweski—or Jerry Press, if you prefer—drank four cans of beer while I worked on one. I told him that he would be doing tremendous service to the cause of Polish independence by taking Minna and me across the border.

He said, "I don't get it. Canada?"

"That's right."

"Where you going? Toronto?"

"Yes." Why complicate conversations with the truth?

"So why not just go?" His brow furrowed. "I mean, somebody wants to go to Canada, what he does is he just goes. Get in your car, or if you don't got a car, well, just get on a bus, or a train, or if you want to take a plane—"

"We tried that," I cut in.

"So?"

"We were recognized. They deported us."

"Deported?"

"That's right."

"No kidding, deported? From *Canada?*"

"Yes, and—"

"You some kind of Communist or something?"

"Certainly not. We—"

"I mean, the hell, deported from *Canada* for chrissake. What did they try and do, send you to Italy?"

It was a tedious conversation. Jerzy's commitment to the cause of Polish independence seemed highly theoretical. Just as single men in barracks don't grow into plaster saints, neither do beery clods in bowling shirts contribute much to the ranks of conspirators. The liberation of Poland was something for him to drink toasts to at Polish weddings, in case they ever ran out of other things to drink to, which probably never happened. The cause, too, was something for which raffles were held and money raised, something to which prospective congressmen pledged undying support if they wanted to carry Cheektowaga, something that everyone favored but evidently no one was ever forced to do anything much about.

So Jerzy drove his bakery truck and plucked his crabgrass from his lawn and drank his beer—you better believe he drank his beer—and, unlike most of his fellows, he actually knew one true-blue revolutionary, Tadduesz, by name. But as far as penetrating at once to the core of an action problem, as far as being instantly ready to come to the unquestioning aid of a fellow revolutionary, he was a little slow on the uptake.

I wasn't getting through to him at all. It was Minna who ultimately made up his mind for him. "If we don't get to Canada soon," she whispered urgently to me, "they'll catch us here."

"Catch you here?"

"We may have been followed, " I said. "If we're captured in Buffalo—"

"Followed?"

"Well—"

"Jesus God," he said. He looked over his shoulder. I don't know why; all he saw that way was the door to his own house. "One thing I don't want," he said, "is to get involved."

"I don't know where we can go, really. You're our last chance."

He looked over his shoulder again. I wondered if it might be a nervous tic. "I gotta start the bakery route in a couple hours. The customers don't get their bread and rolls on time, they can make a lot of trouble. You wouldn't believe it."

Ah, a spirit filled with revolutionary zeal. "I suppose we could wait here until you're done—"

"Jesus, that's all I need. You and the kid getting arrested here, in my house, with a fifteen-year mortgage still on it, that's just what I need. Listen a minute, I could run you across the Peace Bridge. There's Fort Erie, Crystal Beach, you could get a bus there."

"Just so we get across the border."

He drove us there in a year-old Dodge station wagon. He took the spare tire out of its well and put our suitcase in its place, then filled the station wagon's luggage compartment with bathing suits and towels. "We tell them we're going to Crystal Beach," he said. "Just for the day, just to go swimming, see? We don't want 'em to see no suitcase. Got it?"

We had it.

"They'll ask, you know, where you were born. Say Buffalo. I always say Buffalo. Lodz I was born in, you think I'm going to say Lodz when they ask me? I should show 'em proof of naturalization, all that crap? I say Buffalo, I speak good English. You do it the same way. Where were you born, you say Buffalo. Buffalo, New York, even. That's how you can say it, or just Buffalo. I just say Buffalo most of the time. Don't matter."

He drove us through the heart of the city to the Peace Bridge entrance on the lower west side. We crossed the Niagara River, and a Canadian guard asked us where we were born. Jerzy was shaking as if suffering from Parkinson's Syndrome. We all said that we were born in Buffalo and we were all evidently believed. Jerzy announced that we were going to Crystal Beach and would be back by nightfall. No one even looked in our luggage compartment. We drove on into Canada.

"This here's Fort Erie," Jerzy said. "I think you can get a bus from here to Toronto. The downtown's over this way, I'll see if we can't find the bus station and—"

And the tire blew.

Of course the spare was in the garage in Buffalo. I had begun anticipating a blowout the moment he went through his act with tire and suitcase, and had merely hoped the tires would hold until we crossed the bridge. "Wait here," I told him. "I'll pick up a tire at the nearest gas station and help you change it. Do you know the tire size offhand? I—"

"No." He was shaking his big head with great determination. "You just go on," he said. "You just take the suitcase and go on, you and the kid. I can manage myself with the damn car."

"But—"

"Listen, all I want is the two of you the hell out of the car and out of the house. Money is one thing, a donation is one thing, but I could lose my job, I could get in all kinds of trouble. You get the suitcase and you keep walking that way and you get a bus."

He was being ridiculous, but it was his car and his problem and, the border safely crossed, no longer mine. I reached out a hand. "You are a good comrade, a faithful worker," I began.

"You crazy man, speak English!"

"And Poland thanks you," I concluded in English. I took the suitcase with one hand and Minna with the other, and we left him there. Downtown Fort Erie was not of sufficiently great size to make the bus station hard to locate. It sat there on the main street. We had to wait three hours for the next Toronto bus, and could make good connections there for Montreal. I bought tickets and sat down next to Minna.

"Why did we need him?" she asked, reasonably.

"He got us across the border."

"Could we not have walked across?"

"Perhaps. He seemed like a good idea at the time."

"He was a very nervous man, Evan."

"Yes. That was a good idea of yours, somebody chasing us."

"Thank you. I did not know if it was the right thing to say, but I thought it was funny how nervous he was and that perhaps we ought to make him be more nervous."

Evidently Jerzy's nervousness was contagious. We were almost monotonously safe by that time, but I couldn't entirely avoid stiffening automatically every time a policeman entered the bus station. I bought Toronto and Montreal and Buffalo newspapers, partly to read and partly to hide behind. Minna, bless her, closed her blue eyes and slept.

4

ur hotel was not exactly that. All the advance planning in the world could not have prepared Montreal for the task of housing the horde of visitors drawn by the fair, and the citizens of the city had responded to the challenge by renting out broom closets, bathrooms, and back porches at staggering rates. We had been comparatively lucky, working our way east on St. Catherine Street from the center of the city into an area on the periphery of the old French quarter, ultimately finding a large room with a double bed in a building that probably should have been condemned. The rate was twenty-two dollars a night. It was a frightening room and a terrifying price, but by the time we found it, neither the time (late at night) nor Minna's physical state (exhaustion mingling with hysteria) tempted me to go further. We took the room, paid two nights' rent in advance, and Minna fell asleep on the way to the bed. I tucked her in and went outside to have a look at Montreal.

The two-stage bus trip there, via Toronto, was every bit as bad as I had expected it would be. As general rule, I try not to spend more than an hour on any bus, ever. Coming as it did on the heels of three plane rides and Jerzy Pryzesh-weski, this particular trip was less welcome than most. The roads were good, but the bus's shock absorbers were not. The only good thing about the bus was that it got us to Montreal, and I wasn't entirely convinced that that was good, either.

Outside our hotel I turned left and started walking toward the downtown section of the city. It was late, but Rue Ste. Catherine remained brightly lit and thick with pedestrian traffic. There was something very unreal about the area, and it took me a few blocks to realize what it was. Everything looked very American—supermarkets, car lots, stores with exotic names as Woolworth's and Rexall Drugs—but absolutely everything was written in French. This left the place with the air of a *What's Wrong With This Picture?* feature, as unreal as a brace of Beefeaters promenading to and fro in front of the Eiffel Tower.

The city was officially bilingual, of course. So, for that matter, is all of Canada, but outside of Québec one encounters French only on government forms and the like. Here in Montreal, where the city was officially 65 percent French —probably a low estimate—an overwhelming Gallic accent predominated. Some stores had signs only in French, others supplied English signs as well, but French was always the major language.

I walked through the streets, letting my ear accustom itself to the language around me. Québec French is not nearly as much of a corruption of the original tongue as a Parisian would have one believe. A Cornishman and a Northumbrian Geordie, both of them living in England itself, would have considerably more difficulty communicating than would a Montrealer and someone from the French mainland. There is a distinct Canadian accent, certainly, a definite tone and rhythm to Québecois speech, but anyone who speaks French and has any kind of ear for languages can pick it up in a hurry.

I let myself hear the language and forced myself to think in it—if you can't think in a language, you don't really have it down yet—and as I did this, stopping at a lunch counter for a smoked meat sandwich, stopping at a tavern for a glass of wine, an odd thing happened.

I found myself becoming very firm on the subject of Québec autonomy.

As a matter of fact, I had almost forgotten about that particular cause until the border clowns at the airport had forced it upon my attention. Some causes make more noise than others, and the MNQ had been lately quiet. A few years back, when some loyal activists had been using plastique to blow hell out of mailboxes, I had been more firmly committed. (Anyone who fails to find beauty in the systematic demolition of mailboxes has no soul.) But things were quiet, and there was little MNQ activity in New York, and, if I had not precisely lost interest, at least the extent of my emotional involvement had receded.

All changed, changed utterly. I lifted a glass of red wine in a silent pledge to Québec Libre. I ordered a second glass of wine and looked at the mob of convivial drinkers around me. Two hundred years of subjection had not altered them. Generations had come and gone, yet all of my fellow drinkers not only spoke French—they *looked* French. Obvious the Canadian Confederation had to be torn apart. Obviously these men deserved their freedom. Obviously—

I left the bar without having a third glass of wine. This was probably a good thing. Already inflammatory slogans were sloshing around in my brain, and another glass of the dry red wine might easily have moved them to my lips. I was not even supposed to be in the damned country, and the reason for my presence had nothing whatsoever to do with the heroic struggle for a free Québec, and the last thing I wanted to do was call attention to myself.

Further downtown it became easier to resist the siren's song. In the heart of the commercial district the aura of French culture was far less prevalent. Everything down there was incredibly new, with the great majority of the buildings less than five years old. Skyscrapers, all glass and steel, thrust themselves geometrically into the air. Movie theaters and strip clubs and restaurants and bars were far more reminiscent of Broadway than of anything

French. I had another smoked meat sandwich—it's like pastrami—and drank innumerable cups of coffee.

At least it was cool out, cooler than New York. I still didn't want to be in Montreal, and I still couldn't believe that the fair was going to be much fun, and I didn't even want to think about my reconnaissance mission at the Cuban Pavilion. But there were no race riots going on, and no air pollution, and my landlord was 400 miles away, as in fact was all of New York. And, by God, it was cooler.

I hoped it would stay that way. Because our sad excuse for a room wasn't air-conditioned.

By the time I got back to the room, the sun was up and Minna wasn't. She had managed to sprawl diagonally across the double bed. I had to rearrange her in order to stretch out next to her. She didn't even stir. I lay flat on my back and closed my eyes and went through the Yoga routine of relaxing each group of muscles in turn, then turning my mind off by thinking of nothing, which is harder than it sounds. I stayed that way for some twenty minutes. When I yawned and stretched and got out of bed, I didn't feel tired anymore. I selected clean clothes and climbed a flight of stairs to the bathroom. There was no shower, just a disreputable tub. First I washed the tub, and then I filled it and entered it and washed me. I returned to our room and woke Minna and sent her up for a bath. She was back again in less than ten minutes, desperately anxious to get to the fair before they closed it. I told her they hadn't even opened it yet.

We had breakfast, then took a cab to the fairgrounds. The Expo was situated on a pair of islands in the St. Lawrence River. We bought seven-day passports, had something stamped on them, passed through a turnstile, and rode something calling the Expo Express out to the actual Expo site. The train was completely automated and as tightly packed with fairgoers as a rush-hour subway.

Minna kept oohing at things through the window. We passed Habitat, a new approach to urban renewal featuring little concrete cubicles piled tipsily upon one another. We crossed part of the river, stopped at the Île de Ste. Helene, crossed another part of the river to the Île de Nôtre Dame, and left the train.

Nôtre Dame was the location of most of the national pavilions, Cuba included. I managed to establish this by referring to the official Expo map, which someone had sold me for a dollar near the turnstiles. We left the train and climbed down a long wooden staircase and found a bench to sit on, and I studied the map while Minna pointed at buildings, and before very long I gave up and threw the map into a concrete trashbin. It was utterly unintelligible. The site had been divided into four sections, each of which was given a folding map, with numbers all over the map to indicate what everything was, and with the numerical keys buried on the back of other maps, to the point where it became quite impossible to determine where *we* were, much less where anything else was. Once I had thrown the thing away, I was able to look around at the great extent of fairgrounds. I still didn't know quite where we were or quite where the Cuban Pavilion was, but now it didn't much matter.

I had not been prepared for the sheer size of everything. There were massive buildings everywhere, brightly colored structures that clashed dissonantly with one another, extreme architectural excesses, triangles and spheres and palaces and tents, most of them pointing up the stated theme of the fair by suggesting that Man and His World were mutually incompatible. The pavilions dominated the scene like dinosaurs astride a prehistoric landscape. Beneath them, scattered among their feet, were the lesser mammals of the age, not nearly as glorious but better suited to survival—the boutiques and souvenir shops and hot dog stands and soda bars that rake in dollars while the pavilions offered themselves free of charge.

Overhead, little blue trains zipped along on the Minirail. Helicopters buzzed here and there. Boats of sightseers cruised the canals. A pedicab rushed by us, the cyclist pedaling furiously in the rear while an old lady sat in the chair and fanned herself with a folded Expo map. At least she had discovered a use for the thing.

There were people everywhere, great mobs of them. They stood patiently in lines stretching out in front of some of the larger pavilions or walked furiously from one place to another. They bought hot dogs and hamburgers and soft drinks and cigarettes and propeller beanies and floppy hats with their names on them and souvenir pennants and many other things that nobody in his right mind would want. They wore sport shirts and slacks, Bermuda shorts, bathing suits, miniskirts. They carried cameras and umbrellas and cameras and infants and cameras and shopping bags and cameras. God must have loved the fairgoers; he certainly made enough of them. An average of nearly a quarter of a million visited the fairgrounds every day, and at least that many passed in front of us in less than ten minutes.

"It's cool here," I said.

"It is getting warm in the sun, Evan."

"It's cooler than New York."

"Yes, it is."

"That's something."

"Is it not beautiful, Evan?"

"I suppose so."

She stood up, waving her arms ecstatically. "I am so glad we are finally here," she said. "What shall we do first? Do you want to ride on the Minirail? What pavilions shall we go to? Can I have something to drink?"

We went everywhere, we did everything. We rode on the Minirail and took a ride on the boat, which was called the Hovercraft. We went to more pavilions than either of us could keep track of, passing up the ones with lines in front of them—probably the best ones, naturally—and wandering through endless exhibits, most of which concentrated on depicting the economic progress and industrial potential of the country whose pavilion it was. A little of this goes rather a long way. I saw at least twenty different jars of coffee beans, each with a little signboard explaining that the coffee of this particular country was the best in the world, and while it may be a flaw in my character, coffee beans tend to look alike to me. So do chunks of polished wood—each African nation displayed at least twenty specimens of polished wood, for example, testing even Minna's capacity for boundless enthusiasm.

By noon it was as hot as New York. We had lunch at the Algerian Pavilion, a particularly lovely building with a magnificent tiled floor and native tapestries on the walls. The restaurant was on a glassed-in patio. We had couscous with minced lamb, and it was good but very expensive.

At the Jamaican Pavilion we had banana chips, which look like potato chips and taste like buffalo chips. At the Uganda Pavilion I had a cup of Ugandan coffee ("The best in all the world!"), which tasted like any other cup of coffee. Across the road from the Mauritian Pavilion we saw a young boy fall out of the Hovercraft and into the water. Someone jumped in and dragged him out.

Around three in the afternoon, finally, we stumbled upon the Cuban Pavilion.

I think we must have already passed it several times without noticing it. There was a line in front of it but a short one. We queued up and waited while the uniformed attendant admitted groups of twenty-odd people at a time. Eventually it got to be our turn.

It was different, anyway. You had to say that for it. While all of the other nations were boasting about their progress in catching up with Western civilization, the Cubans bragged of having ripped out the existing social order by the roots. The walls were covered with blown-up photographs of Cuban revolutionary activity, firing squads and submachine guns and sugarcane workers on parade, and everywhere the stern visage of Fidel himself, looking like an unlikely cross between Christ and a bird of prey. An electrified map on one wall provided a year-by-year account of revolutionary activity around the world from the close of World War II to the present day. Slogans and Fidelista oratory covered the walls. It was, all in all, an incredible display.

But what really endowed the entire affair with an aura of surrealistic lunacy was the crowd that walked through those rude hallways. Here marched the American bourgeoisie in full flower, wearing their Bermuda shorts and toting their inevitable cameras, walking and pointing and nodding and smiling, taking pictures, chatting, reacting to the Cuban incendiary barrage much as they had reacted in turn to Ugandan coffee beans and Jamaican banana and Greek statues, swallowing and digesting and moving ever onward, quite unaffected by what they saw.

I had the sudden certain feeling that each batch of twenty tourists would emerge from the building into an interior court, where a group of bearded men in fatigues would stand men and women and children against the wall. And the women would say that their feet hurt, and the children would ask for hot dogs, and the men would point cameras and click shutters while the bearded khaki-clad heroes of the revolution set up a machine gun and mowed them all down. Then the next group would come in, and the next—

I shook my head to banish madness. The Chief, I decided, had sent me on the trail of the wildest goose in history. The Cuban Pavilion was subversive, to be sure. Whoever planned it would have been insulted if one said otherwise. It was preaching revolution. But for all the effect it seemed to be having upon its audience, it might as well have been preaching flight to ostriches.

According to the rumors the Chief had heard, the pavilion was being used as a front for some unspecified operation. I couldn't imagine how; it would have made no more sense than using a whorehouse as a front for the sale of dirty pictures. The place was constantly crowded with tourists and very sparsely supplied with attendants. It couldn't have been less suited to clandestine subversive activity had the walls been made of glass.

I went on walking. Minna's hand had come loose from mine somewhere in the course of things. I glanced around and couldn't see her in the crowd. I let a few people push past me and still didn't see her, then decided she must have gone on ahead while I stopped to read some of the more colorful bits of propaganda. I didn't blame her. I followed the crowd to the door and out into the sunshine.

And I didn't see her anywhere.

I called her name a few times and wandered around looking for her. She didn't seem to be anywhere. I bucked the tide of tourists and worked my way back into the building and still couldn't find her. It took me five minutes to locate an attendant and ask him about a little lost blonde girl.

"*No hablo Inglés,*" he said.

I did not believe this at all. I repeated the question in Spanish and he shrugged limply and walked away. I went outside again. I investigated a row of hot dog stands and souvenir booths over to the right of the pavilion. Minna wasn't there. I doubled back to the Cuban Pavilion restaurant and bar, thinking she might have followed part of the crowd there. The headwaiter wouldn't let me in, insisting he didn't have a table for me. I told him my problem and he smiled blandly and assured me that no little girl had come in all afternoon. I shoved him out of the way and looked for myself and couldn't find her.

I went back to the line in front of the pavilion. I waited for fifteen minutes until the attendant let me into the building. I walked all the way through, looking for her everywhere. There was no false route she could have taken, no place she could have hidden herself. I left the pavilion again and walked around it three times, looking everywhere for her. No luck.

Minna was lost.

5

think the helicopter pilot was drunk. His eyes wandered in and out of focus, and he had a disconcerting habit of looking over his shoulder instead of paying much mind to where we were going. The network of capillaries around his nose further suggested a fondness for alcohol, as did the aroma of good Canadian whiskey that issued from him. All of this might have bothered me a good deal more if I hadn't already been too bothered about Minna to pay much attention to him.

"Usually give people a full tour," he was saying. "All the pavilions, the rides, give you the whole feel of the fair."

"Just keep going around in circles."

"Makes a person dizzy."

"Ever-increasing concentric circles," I said. "She went into the damned building and she isn't in it now. Must have come out of it. Keep circling, she has to be here somewhere."

"Dizzy," he said, turning to me and gesturing with one hand. "Dizzy as a dean."

I tried to ignore him. I wished he hadn't kept mentioning dizziness; a helicopter is sufficiently disorienting when it moves in a straight line, and I was beginning to feel overcome by a well-nigh irresistible desire to vomit. I kept my eyes on the ground, amazed that there could be so many people down there without any of them being Minna.

She was usually very good about not getting lost or, failing that, at arranging to get found again. Now, whirling uncomfortably in the air, the helicopter's propellers roaring madly overhead, I wondered if it might not have been a better idea to have kept both feet on the ground. It was the idiot Cubans who had made me blow my cool. Obviously Minna had simply wandered away. Given time and opportunity, she would wander back. But the staccato rattle of violence that the Cuban Pavilion projected had evidently left its mark on me. Even as I thought it all out, I couldn't entirely dismiss the notion that something horrible had happened.

"She could be at the Lost and Found," my pilot said.

"Where's that?"

"Admission gates. People turn in glasses and umbrellas and binoculars and children. Always have a lot of kids there. You just go on down and pick out one that looks right to you." I had to look at him to be certain he was joking. "The things they find. In the morning, you know, they sweep up at La Ronde, that's where the amusements are, where the young kids hang out, why they'll come up with a ton of bras and such. The whole world's going around in circles. It makes a man dizzy."

We banked wildly—I think he was gesturing with the helicopter as less mobile men do with their hands. I placed both of my own hands upon my stomach and coaxed it back into place.

"Took two kids up the other day, I don't believe either of them was a day past sixteen, well, you won't believe what went on in the back there. You know, I just took a peek to see what was going on"—he craned his head toward the rear of the craft, holding the copter on a collision course, aiming dead center at the top of the British Pavilion—"just took a peek, wouldn't you know, and I decided to shake 'em up a little, have a little fun with them, see? So just as they're going at it hot and heavy, you know kids, how they get all wrapped up in what they're doing"—the idiot was still glancing reminiscently at the rear of the plane; the British Pavilion still loomed menacingly in front of us— "why, I just gave the wheel a wrench like this, do you see, just like this, and if that didn't bounce them around some!"

And he gave the wheel a wrench, do you see, and we veered to starboard and missed the apex of the pavilion rather narrowly. I promptly threw up and didn't even mind, deciding it was better than dying.

"I think we'd better go down," I said.

"Now I've gone and made you ill. Clumsy of me."

"If you could drop me near the Lost and Found—"

"Want to have another quick look around first? There's time."

"I don't think so."

Minna was one of the few children in the area who was not at the Lost & Found booth. The small frame structure overflowed with small boys and girls, who in turn overflowed with tears. All of this bedlam was presided over by a young woman with light blonde hair, freckles, and a look in her eyes that suggested that at any moment she might break under pressure and go stark raving mad. And it might have been fun to watch her do so. But while I was there she remained as brittly calm as a hurricane's eye, holding a tissue to this nose, patting that head, cooing to one little wretch while inhibiting the vandalism of another. Had I been somewhat less distressed, I might have fallen in love with her.

"I'm sure your daughter will turn up," she assured me. "They all do, you know. One after another."

"One minute she was there," I said, "and the next minute she wasn't."

"They're like that."

"Yes."

"And they almost always get here before the parents. That's what's so amazing. As if the parents don't even notice they're gone, oh, sometimes for hours."

I didn't think it was that amazing.

"There *is* a baby-sitting service, you know." She wrinkled up her forehead. "Unless some of them feel guilty about actually abandoning their children, but once they're lost, you know, then they want to take advantage of it. Do you think that could be it?"

"It's possible."

"So actually it's rather unusual that you found your way here before your daughter. It doesn't often happen that way."

"Well, I took a helicopter."

"Did you? Oh, my. You certainly are a conscientious father, aren't you?" She separated two potential assassins, then sighed and brushed her hair out of her eyes. "Have you had her paged? You might do that."

"Where do I go?"

"That tent over there, do you see it? I don't suppose it's audible for too great a distance, but one never knows what will work and what won't. Stop, Betty. *Stop!*"

I went to the tent and had them page Minna Tanner, requesting her to report at once to the Lost & Found booth. During the next two hours they repeated the message perhaps a dozen times, during which time I learned that the girl at Lost & Found was named Myra Teale, that she came from Hamilton, Ontario, that she was a divorcée, and that she had no children. I suspected that it would be a very long time before she ever had children on purpose.

Throughout this stretch of time I remained generally anxious without doing too much out-and-out worrying. Anxiety is essentially a passive state that can be endured indefinitely—modern living very nearly demands as much—but actual worrying is far too active a process to be carried on for great stretches of time. I suspect, for example, that those people who insist they spend all of their time worrying about the bomb or pollution or mongrelization of the race or whatever are guilty, at the least, of semantic inaccuracy, if they are not genuine liars. No one can spend very much time worrying about the bomb; one either lives anxiously in its shadow or limps off to the land of Catatonia.

Hell. I spent two hours not exactly worrying about Minna, and not successfully paging her, before reaching two conclusions—that Minna was unlikely to appear at the Lost & Found booth, and that Myra Teale was far too harried to respond favorably to an offer of dinner, or some such. So, for that matter, was I.

Minna was more apt to take matters into her own hands than to run to form. The most likely place for her to turn up, I decided, was our hotel. While I had felt compelled to hunt for her, she would feel no similar compulsion to seek me out; instead, realist that she was, she would proceed at once to our room and wait, patiently or not, for me to rejoin her.

I left the fairgrounds, following the signs to Autobus 168, which would carry me back to downtown Montreal. The bus was rather less crowded than the Expo Express and less jolting than the helicopter. I got off at Dorchester Boulevard, took another bus several blocks eastward, and walked a short distance to my hotel.

I did all of this quite automatically, and without paying very much attention to what I was doing or where I was going or what was transpiring around me. I had to look for Minna at the hotel before I did anything else. Whatever happened afterward depended upon whether or not I found her there. Any number of other topics demanded my attention—the Cuban Pavilion, the course of action to be followed, even the eventual method of reentering the United States—but it was pointless to think about these things until I had returned to the hotel and found or not found Minna. So I didn't think of them, and because it was no time for trivia, I did not think of anything else either. I walked and rode and walked with a sort of numb head, and found my hotel, and climbed the stairs, and knocked on the door to our room, and opened it, and found no Minna there.

I went downstairs to ask the landlady if she had been back, but the landlady did not seem to be present. I went outside and looked around, and saw no one I recognized, and went back to the room to wait. I was hungry and spent a few moments weighing my hunger against the likelihood of Minna's returning while I was out eating. It was a few minutes before I thought to leave her a note—when I develop a numb brain, it stays numb for some time—but ultimately this did occur to me, and I began writing a note, and there was a knock at the door.

I jumped up, rushed to the door, yanked it open. I looked where Minna's little blonde head should have been, and what I saw was a massive silver belt buckle. My eyes crawled upward, past a great expanse of red shirt to a firmly chiseled jaw, a hawk nose, a pair of ice-blue eyes, and a Smoky the Bear hat.

"Mr. Tanner—"

"What happened to her? Where is she?"

"Mr. Tanner, I'm Sergeant William Rowland of the Royal—"

"—is she all right?"

"—Canadian Mounted Police. I—"

"*Where's Minna?*"

"I'm afraid I don't know, sir. I—"

"You don't know?"

"No. I—"

"My little girl is missing."

"Yes, sir. I know."

"You don't know anything about her? Where she is?"

"No."

"Then, uh, what are you doing here?"

"I'm afraid I have to place you under arrest, sir."

"Illegal entry," he was saying. "Suspect that's the only charge you'll have to contend with, Mr. Tanner. They've been going easy on subversion and conspiracy charges, especially with regard to foreigners. My guess is you'll just be charged with illegal entry."

"How about mopery?"

He ignored this. "You'll have to come with us now, sir."

"Us?"

"My fellow officer is waiting downstairs."

"Oh. My little girl—"

"Yes, sir. That would be Minna, sir?"

"She's lost."

"I'm certain we'll be able to locate her, sir."

"How?"

"Children do turn up, don't they, sir? If you'll come downstairs with me now, sir . . ."

I turned around. There was a window. If I wanted to, I could make a run for it, crash through the glass, and wait below on the sidewalk for them with a leg or two broken. It seemed foolhardy. They always get their man, anyhow, and if I were going to be gotten, I decided I might as well be intact at the moment of capture.

I followed him down the stairs. Outside, at the curb, another uniformed Mountie stood alongside a splendid pair of chestnut horses. This second Mountie was almost as tall as Sergeant Rowland, who in turn was almost as tall as the horses. He said, "Tanner?"

I nodded. It seemed a little late to deny it.

"Now, that's a bit of luck, isn't it?" he said to Rowland. "No one with him, I don't suppose?"

"Room was empty."

"A shame, but at least we let him go to ground. Not enough to get the fox, you ought to know the location of the foxhole as well. Wonder how many more of the terrorists we'll find in this bloody hotel."

"I just came here, " I said, "because they had a room available."

They ignored me. "Might be worth posting a man here,"

Rowland said. "Might mention as much back at the post."

"Might do."

"How did you find me?"

They looked down at me again. "Left a trail a yard wide, you did," said the one who wasn't Rowland.

"At the fair?"

"At the fair. That page coming over the public address— now, we couldn't honestly miss that, could we?"

I had wondered myself at the advisability of using my own last name when paging Minna, but hadn't seen any enormous drawback. Immigration officers and customs inspectors may have lists of undesirables, and when they do, I am usually on them. But the Expo, even with the cute little passports they gave out, seemed a different sort of proposition.

"And what with your name and picture circulated just this morning all over the country—"

"What!"

"Illegal entry," said Rowland. "Crossed the border at Buffalo-Fort Erie. Why, Fort Erie had it on the wire middle of yesterday afternoon. And I'd say the government had your photograph on file. Don't know as I would have recognized you from it, but with the page and all . . ."

Somehow Jerzy Pryzeshweski had fouled things up. It had not occurred to me that it was unsafe to abandon a Polish truckdriver with a blowout. Evidently the problem of getting back across the border had been insurmountable for him, and he had blown up as thoroughly as his tire.

"Followed you all the way from the fairgrounds, we did," Sergeant Rowland said. "A good thing those buses make plenty of stops en route." He reached up to pat the neck of one of the horses. "Old Chevalier here had himself a merry ride."

"You followed me from Expo on horseback," I said.

"We did, indeed."

"Oh," I said. I looked up at them and at the horses and at the sky. It was warmer than ever. Probably, I thought, as warm as New York. Perhaps even warmer. We need never have left, Minna and I. We could still be there, and in that case I would not be under arrest and Minna would not be lost and—

"Illegal entry," I said.

Sergeant Rowland nodded.

"What will they do to me?"

"Deport you, I'd guess. Wouldn't you say, Tom?"

"Sometimes, now, there'll be a jail sentence, but that's if they should press charges for what you've done in Canada. Not likely, I shouldn't think. Simple deportation for illegal entry, especially what with the Buffalo police pressing for extradition for a more serious crime."

"For a what?"

"Kidnap, wasn't it, Tom?"

"Kidnapping, forcing the victim to convey you across an international boundary, and I'm not certain what else." He smiled winningly. "Don't think you'll have to worry about being kept long in Canada, Mr. Tanner. Just long enough for them to process the paperwork, don't you know, and then ship you back to the Stateside people."

"Of course you'll be questioned, I'd say. Contacts in Montreal and I don't know what. Why, I don't know but that they'll want to know more than a little about your terrorist friends and what they have planned. But you'll be in an American jail before long."

If I ever got out of jail, which seemed less likely by the minutes, I would have to do something about Jerzy Pryzeshweski. Something terminal.

"About the girl," I said.

"The girl?"

"My daughter. Minna."

"Oh, yes."

"I really have to find her," I said. "You see, she disappeared. Here one minute, then gone."

"Of course she's in the country illegally, too—"

"Well, the hell with that," I said. "I just want her with me."

"Turn up soon, I suspect. Think so, Will?"

"They generally do, " Rowland said.

"That's wonderful," I said, "but—"

"Trust they'll take it up with you once we get back to the station. Tom, you lead the way on Chevalier, how's that? And Mr. Tanner and I will follow on Prince Hal."

"Prince Hal is that horse," I said.

"Why, right you are, sir. Now, if you'll just ride up forwards like, not too far up on his neck but leaving the saddle for me, and I'll give you a hand up if the stirrup's not easy for you, and—"

"You've got to be kidding," I said.

They weren't. I have ridden horses before, and I do not doubt that I will do so again, but I would much prefer not to. I don't mind donkeys, nor do I much mind riding on a cart *behind* a horse or a mule or whatever, but bouncing along on top of a horse makes me feel like a horse. Or a part of one, anyway. Sergeant Rowland gave me a hand up, and I landed very unpleasantly with a leg on either side of the beast, and Tom got onto the other horse, and Rowland leaped deftly into the saddle behind me. Chevalier led the way and we followed on Prince Hal, and by this time, as you may well imagine, quite a crowd had collected. I guess the populace had gotten the gist of things, because a few sympathizers shouted "*Québec Libre!*" from the sidelines, and one spectator actually had the effrontery to pelt poor old Chevalier with an egg. Most of the crowd, however, either had no political sympathies for me or preferred to keep them hidden. As far as they were concerned, it was all an interesting spectacle; the cheer they raised was nonpartisan, expressing equal enthusiasm for the Mounties, for me, and for the two splendid, if uncomfortable, animals who carried us.

"Not much of a hand at this sort of thing, sir? If you try to move when he moves, do you see—"

"He bounces," I said.

"A good gait, he has. You move with him, see."

I moved with him whether I wanted to or not. We cut west on Ste. Catherine, moving inexorably toward downtown Montreal. I asked where exactly we were going and Rowland gave me the address, but it didn't do me much good; it was a street I hadn't heard of before. It didn't really matter, I decided. Uncomfortable as the ride might be, the next few days or weeks or months promised to be considerably less comfortable.

I couldn't take the kidnapping charge seriously; Jerzy would withdraw that soon enough, one way or the other. But there was still enough potential doom in the air without it. And Minna's absence, I decided, was far more sinister than

I had at first realized. Perhaps the Cubans had machine-gunned her in the courtyard. Perhaps the Argentineans had kidnapped her for the white slave trade. Perhaps some agents from the Lithuanian Soviet Socialist Republic had recognized her as the rightful Queen of Lithuania. Perhaps someone from the Israeli Pavilion wanted to use her blood to make unleavened bread. Perhaps—

Hell. I had accepted the Cuban Pavilion assignment, after having been provided with every possible opportunity to cop out. Now it was impossible to carry it out. Everything had already gone wrong, and once I disappeared inside whatever sort of fortress the Royal Canadian Mounted Police maintained for American kidnappers, I would be completely out of control; even more things could go wrong, and there wouldn't be anything on earth I could do about them.

There is a sort of situation in which the thinking processes quickly wither utterly away, leaving in their wake an animal who lives wholly in the present and responds automatically and instinctively. And so, though I would rather prefer to say that I planned what happened next, I can honestly make no such claim. It sort of happened.

We were approaching the intersection of Ste. Catherine and Rue de la Something. The light was green. Chevalier and Tom had already crossed the intersection, and we were moving into it, Prince Hal and Rowland and I. I was perched on the horse's neck and feeling like one, and Sergeant Rowland had one arm over my shoulder, the reins in his hand, and Prince Hal, for his part, was proceeding at what I guess was a brisk trot.

So I grabbed the reins in one hand and tugged back hard, and then I dropped them momentarily to take Rowland's arm in both hands, one at the elbow and the other back near the shoulder. I couldn't really get my back into the maneuver, but the sudden cessation of forward movement on Prince Hal's part made up for what I lacked in leverage, and I supplied a sort of pivotal movement with my shoulders and ducked my head and threw up and out with both arms, and Sergeant William Rowland of the RCMP sailed over first my head and then Prince Hal's head before landing upon his own.

I sort of bounced backward, aiming for the saddle. This didn't work as well as it might have—I hadn't remembered about the saddle horn—but I did wind up in the right place. I snatched up the reins in my right hand. I'm not sure which hand you're supposed to hold the reins in, if it matters. I aimed my feet at the stirrups and couldn't reach them. So I pulled Prince Hal's head around sharply to the right, and I kicked my unstirruped feet into the sides of his rib cage, and the noble beast took off down Rue de la Something as if someone had told him the randiest mare in creation was waiting at the next corner.

I held on for dear life. If I had planned all this, I might have begun praying, but it didn't occur to me.

6

One of the few nice things about a horse is that it is no more likely to ask questions than an automobile and is almost as apt to do what you want it to do. Prince Hal behaved commendably. With the shouts of onlookers echoing around us, with cries of *"Halt!"* to our rear, and with even an occasional gunshot whistling overhead, Prince Hal put his ears back and galloped for his life. And for mine.

It's possible, of course, that he just plain felt like a good run. I don't suppose a Mountie's mount gets too many chances to run flat out in downtown Montreal. Nevertheless, Prince Hal acted as if he knew just what this was all about. The shouting didn't bother him, the shots didn't bother him, the cars and trucks on either side didn't bother him, and not even the awkward idiot on his back could throw him out of stride. We ran straight for three blocks, at which point I yanked the reins again. By this time I was able to think straight, so of course I did it wrong; I wanted Prince Hal to go to the left, but jerked his head to the right by mistake, and off we went. He executed the turn neatly enough, though. We wound up going the wrong way on a one-way street, but no one gave us a ticket.

I turned around. The still-mounted Mountie, Tom, was in full pursuit, but we seemed to be drawing away from him. Chevalier was no Prince Hal. I could hear an assortment of sirens, but if there were any squad cars actually in view, I didn't notice them.

If we could just shake loose, then we might have a chance. It was pretty obvious where I would have to hide. With all of Canada looking for me because of my Mouvement National de Québec activities, the only people I could trust to hide me were the MNQ bunch. I knew names and addresses and if I could get to one of them, I was safe.

If. If Prince Hal had had wings, we could have flown. In the meantime every siren in Montreal was baying at me like a pack of fox hounds. They were on all sides, from the sound of it, and I had as much chance of going to ground in some terrorist basement as I had of turning Prince Hal into a reincarnation of Pegasus.

Until suddenly a traffic light went red in front of us, and cars hit their brakes, and everything prepared to go smash. I did the only thing possible under those circumstances. I closed my eyes.

Whereupon Prince Hal showed the full extent of his prowess. Somewhere in his ancestry there must have been a winner of some remote Grand National, for the blood of the steeplechase horse flowed in his veins. Mane flying, ears back, he left the ground with incredible grace, a fore-foot ever so neatly staving in the roof of a Ford sedan, a hind hoof just barely poking a hole in the windshield of a Buick convertible. We had no sooner touched the ground than he leaped a second time. This was a capital idea on his part, since our first landing had deposited us in the center of the intersection with any number of cars bearing rapidly down upon us. But Prince Hal made his second leap, sailing right over one of the menacing cars and on past the others, and away we went.

For the first time in my life I understood all those movies that concluded with Randolph Scott kissing his horse. I felt like kissing Prince Hal. He not only had saved us, but he had performed the neat trick of utterly routing our enemies. I looked back, over my shoulder and his tail, at the vehicular carnage behind us; I looked back, and I watched cars hitting other cars, and I was so awed by it all that I very nearly fell off the horse. Prince Hal had directly damaged two cars, and he had scared hell out of the drivers of any number of other cars, with the result that they had all driven into one another. The squad cars could forget about us now. For one thing, they would have to go around the block to resume the chase. For another, they would have their hands full for the time being quelling a riot in at least two languages.

I leaned forward like a jockey in the stretch. I don't know what jockeys whisper to horses. I whispered, "Good horse," which seemed a little bland. If one talks to Prince Hal, I thought, one might as well quote Falstaff. "'I have peppered two of them,'" I said. "Well, you have, anyway. 'I tell thee what, Hal, if I tell thee a lie, spit in my face; call me horse.'"

In the old French Quarter of Montreal, people have houses in their backyards. The houses are built one beside the other and one in back of the other, and a look at them shows just how far we have advanced in the past three hundred years. Now we do the same thing and call it low-income public housing.

I was on foot now. Once we had outrun our pursuit, Hal was rather more a liability than an asset; I wanted to merge with my surroundings, and it is difficult to remain inconspicuous while mounted upon the back of a runaway horse. I tugged the reins, gradually this time, and Hal slowed to a stop, and I got off. Two small boys were playing at the curb. They were delighted to see the horse. I tucked the reins into the hand of one of them and told him to take good care of the horse. He asked if he could keep him forever and ever, and I told him he would have to ask his mother; if it was all right with her, it was all right with me.

I spent the next little while trying to do what I could about the outward appearance of one Evan M. Tanner, Fugitive. For a few dollars a French-speaking wino agreed to my offer of new clothes for old. He was exactly my size, so his clothes were just as baggy on me as they had been on him. I began itching even before I put them on. He was almost as reluctant to part with his cap as I was to dirty my head with it, and I had to throw in an extra two dollars for the filthy thing, but once I'd clapped it on my head, I felt considerably more secure. I checked my reflection in a store window and found that I did not look very much like myself. I certainly didn't smell very much like myself or like anything human.

A few days' worth of beard and mustache wouldn't hurt, I decided. I tried to obtain the same general effect by rubbing dirt on my face, but this didn't work too well. Maybe I wasn't using the right sort of dirt. At least I wound up with my face and hands as filthy as my shirt and trousers and jacket and cap.

I think the clothes helped. It was not merely that I looked and smelled like a wino, but that, garbed as I was and reeking as I did, I damned well *felt* like a wino. Perhaps Stanislavski knew whereof he spake. I henceforth began walking like a wino, with the same rolling gait, the same slow, hesitant movement. I had to ask direction en route, and I slurred my words like a wino, and if I didn't have the Québecois accent down pat, the mumbling covered it. No one wanted to spend any time with me—my odor guaranteed as much—but neither did anyone seem to suspect that I was anything but the cruddy old bum I pretended to be.

The sun was on its way out by the time I reached the old

quarter. I found Rue des Poissons (which had, as far as I could tell, no fishmarkets upon it, its name notwithstanding) and managed to locate the address where Emile Lantenac received his mail. I didn't know if he lived there or not, or if anybody lived there, but Emile was quite important in the MNQ and he and I had met before, and got along well.

His building was three houses back from the street. I made my way to it, drawing more attention than I wanted on the way; the district was quite respectable, albeit ancient, and I was shuffling along looking like a horrible example from a training film on venereal disease. *This Man Was Ravaged by Syphilis*, that sort of thing.

I found Emile's building. I shuffled down a flight of steps to the basement entrance. The door window was obscured by a thick accumulation of grime; it looked rather like I felt.

There was a doorbell. I poked it, but I wasn't sure that anything had happened. I couldn't hear it ring within. I knocked on the door, loud. Nothing happened. I knocked again, louder, and nothing happened again. I put my ear against the window and listened very carefully for sounds within the darkened basement. I couldn't make out anything. I knocked one last time, listening intently.

Nothing, nothing at all.

I used a finger to wipe grime from my ear. There were other names and addresses I knew, other places I could seek shelter, but now that I had managed to reach Emile's quarters, I wasn't happy with the thought of returning once again to the streets. I had the feeling, too, that I might have gone somewhat overboard with my protective coloration. I now looked so disreputable that I might get arrested by mistake.

If Emile still used the basement, sooner or later he would turn up. And, if it was now abandoned, at least it would be a place to hide for the time being, whether anyone ultimately came to my rescue or not. I listened again at the door, and again I heard nothing, and then I looked over my shoulder in the traditional furtive fashion of someone who is about to commit something illegal. No one was looking my way.

I tried the door. It was locked. I put a little muscle into it and couldn't break the lock that way. I took off my jacket and my shoe, wrapped the latter in the former, and broke one of the panes of glass. I opened the door from the inside, then hopped in with my jacket and shoe still clutched tight in my hand. I drew the door shut behind me and stood motionless in the darkness.

The sound of glass breaking did not seem to have drawn any attention. I stood silently, one shoe off and one shoe on, feeling like diddle diddle dumpling, my son John. It was impossible to see anything in that inky gloom. I fumbled around for a light switch and couldn't locate one. I took a step away from the door, and another, and someone took me by the shoulders and pulled me forward.

I stumbled. Other hands lay hold of me. I said "What—" and a hand fastened itself over my mouth. I tried to wrestle free. It was useless; my arms were held, and somebody had an arm around my ankles. I went limp and let them ease me back onto the floor.

I could see nothing in the darkness. Then suddenly there was a light, but it didn't do me a bit of good. It was beamed straight into my eyes, blinding.

In French a voice said, "He reeks of the sewer."

"Who is he, then? Just a sot?"

"Perhaps."

"Nnnnnnnn," I said through my nose.

"Throw him out."

"First render him unconscious. What an extraordinary odor! We must get him out of here."

"Nnnnnnn!"

An arm briefly interrupted the flow of light. Overhead, a hand held a leather-covered sap. Like a dog, I bit the hand that muzzled me.

"The bastard has bitten me!"

"Hit him! Knock him out!"

"Emile! Emile, for the love of God!"

The sap stopped halfway to the crown of my head. "*Mon Dieu,*" said an increasingly familiar voice. "Can it be—"

"For the love of God and the glory of Québec, Emile—"

"Evan? It is you?"

"It is I."

Another voice cut in. "You know this wretch, Lantenac?"

"Fool! It is Evan Tanner, the comrade for whom the Cossacks have searched."

"In such clothes? And with such an aroma?"

I blinked at the light. Emile said something, and it was turned out and an overhead fixture switched on. I looked around the cavernous basement room at a sea of unfamiliar faces. At my right a tall skeleton of a man was rubbing the palm of his hand.

"I am sorry I was forced to bite you," I said.

"You have teeth like a serpent."

"I trust I did no damage."

"The teeth of a cobra—"

Emile went to him. "The skin is not broken, Claude? No? Then, you will live." To me, he said, "Let me look at you, Evan. Ah, it is really yourself, is it not? I long to embrace you, and yet—"

"I could use a bath and clean clothes."

"Indeed you could. But it is good to see you nevertheless. How did you find us? How did you know to reach us in the first place? We must have developed security leaks of which I am unaware."

"The address—"

"Oh, of course you know of this foul place." He sighed. "But that you should appear at such a crucial moment, that is remarkable. We had heard you attempted to enter Canada and were refused. Then we heard of your illegal entry, and there were rumors the police had captured you—"

"I escaped."

"We had heard that as well, but one is never certain what is to be believed. But it does not matter now, does it? All that is important is that you are here." He lowered his voice. "At a most opportune moment, my old friend. We can make good use of you."

A major propaganda campaign, I thought. A rally, a demonstration. Or perhaps a more dramatic effort. Last time it had been mailboxes; I wondered what would be this month's target.

Emile stepped back and turned to the rest of the group. "This is Claude," he said, pointing to the skeleton. "It is he whom you maimed with your serpent's teeth, but I am sure he will find it in himself to forgive you and that you will not hold it against him for treating you so roughly. In the dark we did not know who you might be, Evan. A police spy—that was the immediate suspicion. They have been very hard on us ever since the Expo first opened."

"I can imagine."

"And do you know any of the others? This is Pierre Martin, I am sure you know his articles, yes? And Jacques Berton, and beside him his brother Jean. And Lucie Gerard, and Carole Phideaux, and Louis . . ."

Emile, his face deeply lined and his hair already white, was the group's senior member. He was not so old as he looked, about forty-five, perhaps. The others were all considerably younger, most of them in their twenties. They were all quite conservatively dressed. The men wore ties and jackets except for Claude, who had on a turtleneck sweater. The two girls, Lucie and Carole, were clean and neat and rather plain.

The third girl was not.

"And this," Emile said, looking at her now, "this is our Jeanne d'Arc, half Angel of Mercy, half Angel of Death. Arlette Sazerac."

If the other girls looked like clerks in Paris shops, Arlette looked like a goddess from the slums of Marseilles. She wore black denim slacks that hugged her slim hips and a green velour top that was drawn out into two appealing points in front. Her face was of the gamin sort, her hair a very dark brown, cropped boyishly short in a ragged soup-bowl cut. A tigerskin beret was perched atop her little head. Green berets make one think of Vietnam. Tigerskin berets make one think of tigers, but Arlette would have had this effect whatever she wore.

"And this," Emile said, pointing to me, "as you know, is our good comrade from the mighty nation to the south. Just as Lafayette assisted the good General Washington in over-throwing British tyranny three hundred years ago, so shall our friend Evan Tanner help us to cast aside the same yoke of oppression. He is a friend of France and a friend of Québec and a very good friend of us all."

"Emile, the police—"

"You are safe with us," he hurried on. "The police do not bother us, much as they try. You will remain with us, you will be hidden by us, and when the hour comes, you will strike with us!"

I thought of Minna. They would have to help me find her, but now was not the time to broach the subject. According to Emile's script, I had come to Montreal to help him. That wasn't quite the way I looked at it, but I could let it slide for the time being.

"Comrade Evan will be at our side," he went on. "Within a week we shall play our part. Within a week the symbol of English despotism will have the temerity to pay us a visit. Within a week, the very personification of our oppression makes her appearance. She will come to celebrate one hundred years of Canadian 'independence.' But it is we who will celebrate—celebrate the beginning of the end of three centuries of slavery!"

"Wait," I said. "You mean the Queen—"

"The noble lady herself," Emile said. "Liz, Betty, Betsy, Bess—so many versions the English have for a single name!" His bright eyes danced. "She will sail down the St. Laurent upon a barge, making her ceremonial visit to the fair. And before she reaches her destination, the Mouvement National de Québec shall kidnap her, with Québecois autonomy as the price of her ransom!"

I guess I gaped. Off to the side a voice said, "Bah!"

I turned. It was Claude. "I have said before and I say again," he snapped, "to kidnap is a game for children. We have had enough of games."

"Claude—"

"To kidnap is foolishness. We have dynamite, we have plastique. Her barge shall sail down the Saint Lawrence like a garbage scow, and we will blow the English bitch to hell!"

A rumble went through the room. I looked at Emile, who looked first at Claude and then at me. Then his face relaxed into a smile.

"As you can see, Evan, we have yet some disagreements on strategy. But they will solve themselves. They are not important now." He placed his leathery hands upon my unkempt shoulders. "You are here, Evan. You are with us. What else matters?"

The tub in which I sat was nearly as deep as it was long. It had claw feet, and I felt that it would come to life if I could only utter the proper incantation. I scrubbed myself diligently with an oval cake of sandalwood soap. A trifle effeminate, perhaps, but anything was preferable to essence of wino.

Arlette's voice filtered through the oak door. "There is ample hot water, Evan?"

"Yes."

"I have put your clothing in the incinerator. I could not abide them in the apartment. You are not angry with me?"

"Not at all. Uh . . . the shoes—"

"I did not burn your shoes."

"Good."

"There is clothing in the closet for when you have finished your bath. I will purchase the newspapers for you now. You wish copies of all of them, no?"

"If you please."

"Evan?"

"What?"

"The English ones as well?"

"Please."

"It saddens me to purchase the English newspapers. Would not the French suffice?"

"I'm afraid not. I have to find out as much as I can, Arlette."

"The French papers are excellent."

"I know that."

"They probably contain all the news that is to be found in the others."

"Even so—"

Her sigh was barely audible through the door. "Very well," she said. "I shall do as you ask. Au revoir."

"Au revoir."

I soaped and washed and soaked, over and over, and I might well have spent eternity in that bathtub, but I wanted to be out and dressed when Arlette returned. I got out, drained the tub, and wrapped up in a large blue towel.

Arlette's apartment, just a few blocks from Emile's conspiratorial cellar, consisted of a large room with a skylight, a kitchen, and the bathroom I had just vacated. The furniture may have been Arlette's or her landlord's, but I suspect that the previous owner was the Salvation Army. The sole note of elegance, and one which contrasted sharply with the pervading Poverty Program flavor, was a tigerskin throw which covered the bed. It wasn't fake anything. It wasn't even real dynel. It seemed to be genuine tigerskin, a perfect match for her beret.

The air was thick with the pungent scent of Gauloise cigarette smoke. I found clean shorts and socks laid out for me on the bed. In the closet there was a variety of male attire, much of it in my size. I found a maroon shirt and a pair of dark gray gabardine slacks. I donned all of these things and was lacing up a shoe when Arlette returned, her arms overflowing with newspapers.

"All of them," she said triumphantly. "The English as well."

"Thank you."

"I behaved poorly before. You must understand, the authorities make use of the circulation figures for the English newspapers. Businessmen must buy them for certain of the business news, and so by presenting circulation figures, the authorities may suggest that the English minority in Montreal is more literate than the French. One does not care to play into their hands, so one avoids buying English papers."

"I understand."

"But what different can these few copies make? This is what I tell myself as I buy them, eh? But you look so much better in clean clothes, Evan. Such a disgrace to have seen you for the first time dressed and perfumed as you were."

She came closer, sniffing. "You smell delightful now. You have used some of my perfume?"

"It was the soap."

"But certainly." She lit a cigarette. "I shall make coffee. Will you be comfortable in that chair? I do not think the light is good. Why do you not make yourself more comfortable upon the bed?"

I stretched out on the bed with the stack of newspapers. I checked through all of them, and for all the good they did me, she needn't have bought the English ones. Or the French ones either, for that matter. They had all gone to bed before my little adventure with Prince Hal, so the only coverage of me dealt with my earlier attempted crossing and my successful illegal entry at Fort Erie. Several of the papers went into some detail on that point. The consensus seemed to be that I had broken into the home of one Jerzy Pryzeshweski, a Buffalo bakery salesman. (No two papers spelled the bastard's name the same way.) I forced him at gunpoint to take us across the Canadian border. Then, in Fort Erie, I left his truck after striking him on the head with the gun butt and slashing his tire to discourage pursuit.

Evidently a cop had happened on Jerry while he was changing a tire, and the clod had panicked instantly and then made up a cover story to protect himself. But it certainly hadn't done me a world of good.

The papers didn't provide the most important thing of all—a lead to Minna's whereabouts. It had occurred to me earlier that some Canadian cop might have snatched her at the fair, thinking that her disappearance might cause me to come out into the open. If that was what had happened, I would hear about it soon; now that they had her, and now that they no longer had me, they would have to use her as bait.

"Coffee, Evan."

The coffee was strong, with chicory added for extra taste, along with a generous slug of cognac for authority. I sat up and sipped it, and Arlette crawled onto the bed beside me, tucked her legs under herself. She drank coffee and smoked another Gauloise. I rather liked the smell of it, but I couldn't understand how anyone could manage to smoke it.

She asked if the papers had been helpful. I said that they had, which was not entirely true, and that we might find more information in the morning papers or on the radio. There was a radio beside the bed. She switched it on and we got the tail end of a Beatles record. *Penny Lane*, I think it was. She said there would be news on the hour. It was then a quarter after ten.

"I hope it will not be necessary to kill the Queen," she said.

I had been trying not to think about all of that.

"Is she a bad woman, Evan?"

"Not at all," I said. "She's rather a good queen, actually. Of course she's a usurper."

"She is?"

I nodded. "They call it the House of Windsor now, but that doesn't really change a thing. It was the House of Hanover when George I took over in 1714, and no matter what Betty Saxe-Coburg calls herself, it doesn't alter the legitimacy of the Stuart claim to the throne."

"And the Stuarts, they still exist?"

"Yes. The French supported the Stuart Pretenders for many years. There's a Stuart Pretender alive today, a

Bavarian Crown Prince, actually." I sighed. "But he doesn't work at it very hard, I'm afraid."

"Do the French support his claim?"

"No. Only the Jacobite League."

"Are you of this Jacobite League?"

"Certainly."

"Ah," she said. "Perhaps one day a reborn France will support Prince—what is his name?"

"Rupert."

"Prince Rupert. Yes."

"Perhaps," I said. "But in the meantime Betty Saxe-Coburg is the best queen England's got. It might not be a good thing if anything happened to her."

"She is only to be kidnapped, Evan."

"Uh," I said.

"It is for the cause. Of course you support the scheme."

"Somebody said something about killing."

"Oh, but that was Claude. He—"

"Dynamite, I heard him say. And plastique."

"Claude is an extremist." Who among us, thought I, is not? "It should not be necessary to do anything of that nature, Evan. I personally favor the kidnapping. It will bring us considerable public attention, will it not?"

"No question about it. But—"

"The eyes of the world will be focused upon the MNQ."

"The guns of the world, too." I sat up straight, looking into her liquid brown eyes. "You can't demand that England grant independence to Québec, Arlette. England has nothing to do with Québec. If Canada wants to dissolve the Canadian Confederation, that's up to Canada. I don't think it will happen as long as the financial community is so closely interlocked, but it's a future possibility and I'm proud to work toward that end. But frankly I don't see how kidnapping poor Betty is going to do any good."

"It will bring us publicity."

"If that's all we want, we could swallow goldfish."

"Pardon?"

"Nothing. Look, the ransom demands cannot be met. Then what happens?"

She shrugged prettily. "That is a bridge we shall cross—"

"After we've blown it up, no doubt."

"Ah, Evan." She rested her head on my shoulder. "But it is not to worry now, do you see? The important thing is that you are here, that you have joined with us. And you will be of help to Emile in countering the influence of Claude. The membership will listen to you—"

"Claude won't. He doesn't much care for me."

"Well, you bit him, Evan."

"I know."

"And he is a very impulsive man. Also a cruel man, you understand? He says that, like all of us, he is a terrorist and a patriot, but at times I think that the terror is more for him than the patriotism. I will get us more coffee."

I waited on the bed for her. I watched her go, buttocks wiggling pertly in the tight denim slacks, and I watched her return, breasts bobbing provocatively in the tight velour shirtlet, and I remembered suddenly how they had all taken it for granted that I should hide myself with Arlette. As though this was standard operating procedure, as though anyone who drifted by in need of sanctuary should be taken to Arlette's comforting bosom.

This had not seemed remarkable at the time. I had simply

assumed that Arlette's apartment was most satisfactory in terms of secrecy and available space. Only now did I realize that, whatever the extent of the secrecy, there was certainly not much in the way of available space. There was just that one room, and there was just the one bed, and although I did not sleep and thus did not need to make use of the bed, why, none of them knew this, and thus they took it as a matter of course that I would share that bed, that Arlette and I would share it, and—

"Your coffee, Evan."

I accepted the cup, held hers too while she joined me on the bed. She settled herself on the tigerskin, and our bodies touched.

"Tigers," I said.

"A noble animal, is it not so?"

"But of course."

Her hand stroked the tigerskin in such a way that I found myself envying the animal. "So bold," she said. "What does the tiger remind you of?"

"Gas stations," I said.

She looked at me. Sometimes I have a lamentable tendency to say the wrong thing. I tried to fight my way out of it.

"And sugar frosted flakes," I said, "and, uh, men's hair tonic, you know. Tigers on your team and in your tank and everything. You know, uh, grrr."

"Gasoline and cereal and hair tonic," she said.

"And you, Arlette."

It was cool now, a rather pleasant night despite the grinding heat of the day. That was one thing about Montreal—it cooled off at night. It was cool then, and quite pleasant, and I thought of Sonya and how little use we had had for each other once my air-conditioner had gone on the fritz. I realized that it had been, actually, quite a while since the air-conditioner died, and quite a while since the thing Sonya and I had had for each other died along with it.

Quite a while, all right.

And I looked at Arlette. Well, here we are, I thought. Here we are, in her room and, uh, in her bed, and everyone sort of assumed I would wind up here—evidently, Arlette included—and—

I said, "La Jeanne d'Arc de Québec."

"Oh, not I, Evan."

"But that was what Emile called you."

"Emile makes jokes. Or perhaps he means that I am like the sainted Joan because I too am the most fervent of patriots." She turned toward me. "I am, you know. My heart pounds in my breast with patriotic zeal."

"I can believe it."

"Right here," she said, pointing.

"Eh."

"Feel it, Evan. You can feel it pounding."

I placed my hand in the center of her chest. "I feel it," I said. "I feel it, all right."

"Not in the middle, cabbage. On the left side. The heart."

"Ah, yes. Yes, I, uh, feel it, uh."

"Evan."

"Uh."

"You smell so much nicer since your bath. I like this aroma."

"It's your soap."

"Yes. Do I smell the same?"

She smelled of luxuriantly strong tobacco and sweet subtle perfume and, yes, sandalwood soap. She tasted of coffee and chicory and brandy. Her hand moved and she said, "Oh, how nice," and I said "Arlette," and we were in rather a hurry. She wrestled the tight black denim slacks down over her hips, and I got out of the slacks and shorts that some obliging man had left behind, and she said "Oh, oh," and I don't remember what I said, if anything. I don't think the earth moved, but that only happens in Spanish sleeping bags, if ever.

"Not Joan of Arc," she said a while later.

"Helen of Troy. Cleopatra. Eve."

She purred. "But not Joan, not the Maid of Orleans. Because, you see, I am not a maiden at all, am I?"

"Not quite."

"But sometimes I do hear voices."

"Oh? What do they say?"

She took me in hand, so to speak. "They say, 'Do it again, do it again!'"

When such voices speak, one obeys.

8

had breakfast ready when Arlette awoke the next morning. I scrambled eggs, buttered toast, browned spicy sausages, and perked coffee. All but the last of these efforts turned out to be superfluous as far as the Unmaid of Orleans was concerned. She grunted unintelligibly, poured herself a cup of coffee, tasted it, made a face, laced it liberally with cognac, and sulked over it in a corner.

Few persons are at their best in the morning. I cannot

honestly recall what it was like for me, the process of waking up, but I do know that it was something I did every day for eighteen years, and I can't believe I could have done it very well. The whole concept of being torn roughly from the fantasy we call dreams to the other fantasy we call reality—what is it, in fact, but the trauma of birth repeated at twenty-four-hour intervals throughout the whole of a person's lifetime.

If I had to pick one reason above all others for treasuring my permanent insomnia, it would be simply this—I never have to give it up.

Arlette did, though, and poorly. I tried to pay as little attention to her as possible for the half hour during which she came gradually to life. This was not only simple courtesy but a matter of personal taste. She was less than charming. Her ragged mop of hair, so charming a few hours earlier, now looked like the coiffure of a small-time Medusa, a nest of lifeless earthworms. Her complexion bordered on jaundice. Her eyes were puffy. And her entire demeanor was the sort only to be viewed in those horror movies in which corpses walk.

Rebirth took half an hour. It was like a death scene—the last act of "Camille," say—filmed via time-lapse photography and then shown backward. The eyes unpuffed, the mouth ungrimaced, the body firmed up, the whole person came back to the land of the living. At last she was sufficiently in control of herself to find her way to the bathroom, from which she emerged as the Arlette I had known and loved (and loved, and loved) just a little while earlier.

"Evan, my heart," she said. "What a beautiful morning!"

It was all of that, bright and warm and clear. "And you

are beautiful, Arlette."

"I am horrid in the mornings. Such beautiful food you created, and I could eat none of it."

"I ate your share myself."

"Commendable. But how could you eat with such an apparition as myself in the room."

"You are always beautiful in my eyes, Arlette."

"And you tell magnificent lies. Did you sleep well, Evan?"

"I have not slept better in years."

"And why should we not be tired, eh?" She chuckled, then turned serious. "But your little girl," she said. "We must act, is it not so?"

I had told her of Minna the night before, somewhere between Acts Two and Three, and she had been madly indignant, wildly anxious about the girl's fate. She had wanted to do something at once, but I pointed out that there was nothing to do before morning, at least as far as Minna was concerned, but that there was something we could do, just the two of us, without leaving the apartment. Shortly thereafter Minna was, for the time being, quite forgotten.

"I meant to get the newspapers," I said.

"You should not leave the apartment. I will go."

"All right."

Once again she purchased all the papers, the English-language ones as well as the French, and once again I worked my way through all of them. There was some marvelous copy about me that Arlette insisted upon clipping. I was presently the object of the greatest manhunt in Montreal's history since François Somebody butchered seven young boys with a straight razor in 1911. I was somewhat relieved to learn, however, that I had not butchered anyone. A dozen persons had been treated for injuries in the auto wrecks Prince Hal had caused, but all but two had been sent home immediately, and those two would live.

So would Sergeant William Rowland, RCMP, although it would be a awhile before he was back on a horse. He had landed on his head, all right, but I guess his Smoky the Bear hat served a purpose, because he came out of it alive. He had a fractured skull, but it takes more than that to impair a Mountie.

Prince Hal had not turned up by presstime. I found this pleasing news, too, and only hoped the little boy was taking good care of him.

And I, I was thoroughly castigated by every newspaper around. It no longer looked as though my capture would result in prompt extradition to the States. The Canadian authorities had a score of their own to settle with me, and charges would be brought against me for everything from subversive conspiracy, malicious mischief, resisting an officer, assault with a deadly weapon (a horse?), and unlawful flight to running a red light and jaywalking. By the time they sent me back to face the kidnapping charge, I would be at least a hundred and fifty-three years old.

It looked as though it would not be a good idea to let them catch me.

It also looked as though the police did not have Minna, did not know where she was, and did not especially care. Almost all of the papers mentioned the girl, referring to her variously as my daughter and my "young female friend"— I suppose they planned to add statutory rape to my list of crimes. The general journalistic opinion seemed to be that

Minna was being cared for by terrorists with whom I was associated, although one scandal sheet—in French, yet—hinted that I had murdered her and floated the body out to sea.

I put the last paper aside and looked up at Arlette, who had been waiting more or less patiently.

"Well?"

"They don't have her."

"Who does?"

I stood up, performed my caged-lion imitation, then turned to face her again. "I keep coming back to those damned Cubans," I said. "I can't think what motive they might have had—"

"Nor could I. After all, she is not the Queen of England!"

She was the someday Queen of Lithuania, but I had not brought this fact to Arlette's attention. She was also my little friend and ostensible daughter, but I had similarly failed to tell Arlette that I was an American agent, much as I had failed to tell the Chief that I wasn't. I had to agree, though, that she was not the Queen of England.

"Let's forget motive," I said. "I have a hunch something funny is going on in the Cuban Pavilion. If she had just gotten lost, she would have gotten found by now. Even if something, uh, bad happened to her"—I did not want to think about this—"uh, they would know by now. I think she must have been kidnapped, and the only place that could have happened was inside that Cuban nuthouse." I began pacing again. "Something's going on there. I walked through the place twice yesterday and couldn't figure it out, but there is sure as hell something going on. If I took another look around—"

"It is impossible, Evan. You would be recognized."

"I could disguise myself—"

"Your photograph is everywhere. Even if you covered your head with a paper sack, you would be recognized. I will go."

"You?"

"Of course. Am I wanted by the police? Am I one to arouse their suspicions? Am I even one who has been within the pavilion? No, no, no. And so why should I not go?"

"You wouldn't know what to look for."

"What would you look for?"

"Well, uh—"

"You see?" She spread her little hands in triumph. "Even you do not know what it is that you wish to find. And so I will go. It is settled."

"You really ought to be careful."

"Of what?"

"Don't do anything, well, unusual."

She smiled reminiscently. "Sometimes I am fond of doing unusual things, cabbage."

"I know."

"Or perhaps you do not regard as unusual—"

"I know, I know."

She stepped close to me. Her hand fastened on my upper arm. It was impossible to believe that just a little while ago she had emerged from bed looking like incipient death. But most people, and especially women, look better entering a bed than leaving it.

"Emile will arrive in an hour," she said. "You do not recall? He wishes to meet with you to plan the arrangements for the Queen." Her eyes flashed. "I know you will develop a brilliant plan, Evan. It is vital to us."

"I know."

"And when he arrives, I will leave. Or perhaps I will go just before he gets here, to the fair. To the Pavilion of Cuba. You follow me?"

"Anywhere."

"Pardon? But Emile will not arrive for an hour, cherished one. If I were in fact Jeanne d'Arc I might choose to spend that hour in prayer, beseeching my Maker for guidance. How I worshipped the Maid when I too was intact! I addressed my prayers to her, I wished to grow up in her image." She shook her head sadly. "And then when I was just fifteen, a boy touched me right here, can you imagine?" I could imagine. "And I had the most extraordinary reaction! And since then, why, I have been a terrible woman! A creature of the Devil himself, do you not agree?"

"The spawn of Satan."

"But certainly." She shook her head again. "Since then I cannot so much as light a candle to Sainte Jeanne. How could I do this? It would shame me. It would be—Evan, do not touch me like that."

"Why not?"

"Because I will have the most extraordinary reaction."

"Well, fine. My own reaction—"

"Ah, but of course! Two portions of eggs, no?"

"It would not have done to let them go to waste."

"Nor would it do to let this go to waste. Let us become unclad, eh?"

And shortly before Emile arrived (and shortly after we

did): "I will tell you this about the Maid, Evan."

"Eh?"

"In a way, I am her superior. I blaspheme, you say?"

"I say no such thing—"

"But my words are true. With all of this, I remain passionately devoted to my country, to my people. But if Jeanne had ever had a taste of this, she would have let France go hang. I swear it!"

Emile brought friends. The Berton brothers, Jean and Jacques. Both were about my height, with wavy black hair, long, straight noses, and sharply defined features. I could not place their accents at first but later learned that they were from Algeria. Though still in their middle twenties, both had fought valiantly with the OAS in a last-ditch attempt to keep Algeria in French hands. Before De Gaulle managed to disunite the two countries, it had seemed that only two possible solutions to the Algerian question existed—one might liquidate eight million Arabs or one million French colons. Jean and Jacques had done their best to bring the former solution into being.

Jean, the older of the two by a year, had annihilated a variety of persons by hurling bombs into markets in the Casbah. Jacques had raided a Moslem hospital, firing Sten gun bursts into bedridden Arabs. They had not exactly played by the Marquis of Queensbury rules, but then neither had the FLN. When The Magnificent Charles began to cool things, both Jean and Jacques did what they could to cool him instead, and failed.

It had thus become imperative for them to leave Algeria and to stay out of France. They went at first to Israel—

though they were not Jews, they were anxious for the opportunity to go on killing Arabs. Their OAS experience, however, had not prepared them for the work of distinguishing between enemy Arabs and the presumably friendly Arab citizens of Israel, and it presently behooved them to find another home. They were now in Montreal; I wondered where they would go next.

"I have brought Jean and Jacques to this meeting," Emile said, "not only because they are experienced and intelligent"—the brothers beamed—"but also because they are among the more levelheaded and peaceable of our contingent."

The brothers exchanged glances.

"They realize the distinction between valid political action and the perpetration of an outrage. While such as Claude—"

"Claude is a fool," Jean said.

"A madman," Jacques echoed.

"It would be sheer folly," said Jean, "to assassinate the Queen."

"Before," said Jacques, "our demands have been announced."

"If they are then refused, it is another matter."

"Then she would of course be killed. She would be tried, found guilty, and executed."

"There is a difference between execution and assassination."

"The difference between planned terrorism and madness."

I looked at Emile, who looked substantially less alarmed than I felt he ought to. If these bright boys were his moderates, I didn't want anything to do with his extremists.

"The longest journey begins with a single step," he said.

"In the wrong direction?"

He sighed. "One takes things a step at a time, my friend. A step at a time. One must not be too intent on working out every little detail too far in advance. The picture can change, is it not so?" He drew on his pipe. "One has a vision, a picture of a bright tomorrow. But it is not sufficient merely to have a vision. One must take steps to achieve it."

"I could not agree more. But—"

"But no. One takes steps. One feels one's way, and when two forks in the road present themselves"—or even one fork, I thought—"one unerringly selects the right path. If the vision is always in sight, if the steps are certain—"

"If anything happens to Mrs. Battenberg, they'll be able to bury Québec in a matchbox."

"Mrs. Battenberg? I do not—"

"Her married name. Before *he* changed it. The hell with it. I'm getting a headache."

"You have been thinking too much." He shook his head in reproach. "It is no time for thought, my comrade. We must plan."

I honored that statement with a moment of silent devotion, and then we did in fact get down to the serious madness of planning Mrs. Battenberg's abduction. One of the OAS lads unfolded a map, and we spread it out on the floor and huddled over it, tracing the route that the regal barge was virtually certain to take, noting the natural defenses that presented themselves, and taking into account everything but the tides and the signs of the zodiac in planning our ambush.

I got rather wrapped up in it.

Well, why not? It was an idiotic game, but it was also, as the gentleman said, the only game in town. If we were going to abduct the Queen of England, the least I could do was make sure the operation went off as well as it possibly could. If nothing else, I could try to ensure her being kidnapped instead of abducted. And I might be able to have her released safely.

And, when you came right down to it, wasn't there a certain appeal, a certain unmistakable beauty, in the notion of kidnapping Britannia's gentle sovereign? I could have a few words with her, no doubt. Not merely about Québec but of other things as well. Like her abdicating in favor of Prince Rupert, for example. Or her restoring the six northern counties to the Republic of Ireland. Or—

Emile was absolutely correct. It was no time to think. It was a time to plan.

When Emile and the Berton Boys left, I made a fresh pot of coffee and rummaged through Arlette's refrigerator and cupboards. Evidently the girl had solved the problem of what to do with leftovers; she chucked them out. I eventually gave up trying to find something already prepared and began improvising a pilaf of rice and onion and raisins. Arlette didn't have many of the right sort of spices on hand—the dish could have done with a bit of coriander—but in cookery, as in secret agentry, one must work with the materials at hand. I ate well and drank more coffee and listened to the radio. The bright, clear, early morning gave way to deadly hot midday. I sat around perspiring, bathed, dressed, and began perspiring some more.

Then Arlette came back with color in her cheeks and a glint in her eye and a spring to her step. A few hours of simple inertia had taken more out of me than she had spent running around in the sun. "Ah, my Evan," she said, and kissed me furiously. "But such a building! Three times I went through the Cuban Pavilion. If only all our membership and sympathizers could be led through that edifice. How formidable! What an inspiration!"

"So the socialist revolution appeals to you?"

"Socialism? I spit on socialism. But what does it matter? It is not the nature of the revolutionary sentiment that makes the pavilion so exciting. It is the fervor of the revolution itself. How dramatically it is portrayed! How the slogans scream at one, how one can hear within one's head the chatter of machine guns and the roar of the bombs. An inspiration, Evan."

"When one is in a revolutionary mood, any revolution will do."

"Precisely." She lit a Gauloise. "It took me until my third visit to overcome the emotional impact of the pavilion. I was transported, I could barely look for whatever it was that I sought. But then the effect of the displays dissipated for me. I was able to observe dispassionately. I think—"

"Yes?"

"You are right to be suspicious of the Cubans."

"What are they doing?"

"I do not know."

"But they're doing something?"

"I am sure of it." She drew on her cigarette. "I cannot tell you why I feel so, but the feeling is undeniable. The way the guards act, the way they glance here and there, something about them. The whole"—she gestured vacantly with both hands—"the entire atmosphere, the aura of the building itself. A sense that there was more to it than met the eye or ear. I am chattering like a silly woman—"

"No. I know what you mean."

"But I did not actually *see* anything. Do you understand?" She hung her head. "I have found out nothing, in truth. Oh, Evan, I am worried about the girl, the poor little thing. It is not a good place to disappear, that pavilion. I sense it, I feel it. Of all the places where one might vanish, that is the last one I personally would select."

I turned from her and walked to the window. It opened on an alleyway. I looked at the blank wall of the building opposite. I seemed to be looking at any number of blank walls lately, I thought. I cursed the Royal Canadian Mounted Police and I cursed Canadian Immigration and Customs and I saved special curses for the immortal soul of Jerzy Pryzeshweski. Minna was out there somewhere, and I ought to be out there looking for her, and instead I was cooped up in an apartment while everything went merrily to hell around me. A hot apartment, at that. A damned hot apartment. If I wanted to spend my time doing nothing, I could have stayed in my own hot apartment in Manhattan.

"You met with Emile, Evan?"

"Yes."

"How did the planning go?"

I gave her a quick rundown on the ambush plans, and she listened more carefully than I spoke, because her heart was in it and mine was not. When I finished, we fell into a listless silence. She took a turn looking out the window, and I went over to the bed and stretched out on it. She came to me, lay down beside me. I did not kiss her.

"My poor Evan."

"That's where she disappeared, there's no question about it. At that damned showplace of the revolution."

"Cherished one."

"And she wasn't lost or strayed. She was stolen. I wonder."

"What?"

I sat up. "Well, maybe they just like to kidnap people. Maybe that's it. It's an ideal setup for it, I suppose. A constant stream of visitors. They can single out the ones who seem to be alone and presumably won't be missed. But—"

"But what?"

"But why?" I said. "Hell." I got to my feet. "If we could both go there," I said. "No, that's out."

"Why both of us?"

"One in front and one at the rear. One to count everyone entering the Cuban building and the other to count everyone leaving it. If more people go in than come out—"

"I see."

"But it would be risky. In order to come up with anything remotely conclusive, we would have to stay at our posts for hours. Even if the police weren't after me, I don't think I could stay in one spot for that much time without someone noticing."

"It would be difficult," she admitted.

"You'd need a couple of people with a reason for being there. Ice cream vendors, something like that. But the concessions are too rigidly controlled, and an ice cream seller would be too busy selling ice cream anyway to keep an accurate count. I don't see—"

"I have it."

"What?"

"The boys."

"Jean and Jacques?" I grinned. "Somehow I don't think so. Their approach would be to storm the pavilion with fixed bayonets. They'd be very good at it, too, but I doubt that—"

"Not them. Seth and Randolph."

"I don't remember them."

"You do not know them. They are not of the movement. They are Americans, like yourself. They—"

"It might not be a good idea to bring in any Americans, Arlette."

"But they are different. They are—how do you call it? They run from the cold."

"Huh?"

"Pardon. From the draft, the conscription."

"Draft-dodgers?"

"But certainly." Her face took on a dreamy expression. "They are idealists, but of course, and very young and very sweet."

"You know them rather well, Arlette."

"But yes," she said, and glanced involuntarily at the bed.

"Both of them?"

"They are my very fine friends."

"Joan of Arc."

"Ah, but it is only you I love, Evan." She tucked her arm in mine. "I will call them. They will be perfect, I know they will. They can remain in one spot for hours and no one will pay them the slightest bit of attention. Better than the sellers of ice cream."

"How?"

"You will see."

She made a telephone call, telling the boys to come at once and bring their signs. I didn't know what that meant, but before long they appeared and I found out.

Seth, the taller of the two, had brooding eyes and a full red beard. Randolph had shoulder-length hair and a scraggly mustache. And each wore a sign, sandwich-board affairs that covered them front and back from their shoulders to their knees. Randolph's sign said, *Hey, Hey, LBJ, How Many Kids Did You Kill Today?* Seth's read, *God Damn, Uncle Sam, Bring The Boys Home From Vietnam!*

"I see what you mean," I told Arlette. "Perfectly inconspicuous. Who would give them a second glance?"

9

Around nine o'clock that night Seth and Randolph came to Arlette's place a second time. They had disposed of the sandwich boards this time, and brought instead a paper sack of smoked meat sandwiches and a large bottle of Alsatian wine. We talked between bites and gulps, and by the time the food and wine was gone, I had the story.

The Cubans were stealing people.

They couldn't tell me why, and I couldn't guess, but the fact remained that in a period of some four hours eight more persons had entered the Cuban Pavilion than had left it. The two draft-dodgers had equipped themselves with hand-counters, made sure they started and finished at the same time, and were absolutely certain of their tally. They had no way of knowing who those missing eight persons were, whether they might be male or female, young or old, Canadian or American or whatever. But eight had gone in who had not come out, and that was what I had wanted to find out. Minna was not an isolated case but one of many. The Cubans were stealing people.

And presumably, tucking them away somewhere inside their blasted pavilion.

"You did good work," I told the two. "I'm very grateful."

"No sweat," Seth said.

"We go out there all the time anyway," Randolph put in. "With our signs, and like that. You can stand in one spot until the world freezes and nobody makes any waves. We're like part of the scenery."

"No one gives you an argument?"

"Sometimes sombody'll whisper, 'Keep the faith, baby,' or something like that. Or officials from some of the pavilions will ask us to move on. I guess they don't want to jeopardize their country's share of foreign aid. But Cuba was no problem at all. They don't get any foreign aid from us."

"And they're pretty close to our own line on Vietnam," Seth added.

I thought they might encounter harassment from American tourists, but they insisted that wasn't the case. "Some of them agree with us, though they don't want to get caught saying so. Probably eighty percent of them don't much care one way or the other, just so their room is air-conditioned and the television set works."

"The apathetic majority," Randolph said.

"You know it. And the ones who would just as soon stick bayonets in us, well, they have to cool it, see? Because for all they know, we could be Canadians, in which case they would be starting an international incident and they might get called down at the next Rotary Club meeting for conduct unbecoming a clod. Some of them, the real flag-wavers, they get very uptight about the entire scene. I mean, it's comical to watch them. They want to say something, or start swinging, and you can like feel their eyes, trying to read whether we're Americans or Canadians or what the hell we are. My beard and Randy's hair, that just worried them that much more."

The two of them did more than parade around wearing signs. Each of them put in several hours a week at the office of a pacifist organization on Front Street, stuffing envelopes, proofreading newsletters, and otherwise campaigning against war in general and the Vietnamese operation in particular. They devoted the greater portion of their time to encouraging American college students to come north to avoid the draft.

"We get accused of copping out," Seth said. "You know, like we should either join the army and kill a commie for Christ or spend five years in Leavenworth for our principles. I think this is more active, you know. Martyrdom is for masochists." He shrugged. "But a lot of the time I think, well, why hack the whole thing? Send out newsletters, and the only people you impress are the ones who already agree with you. I mean, if you stop to think things out, what good does any of it do?"

"If everybody stopped to think things out," I said, "no one would get out of bed in the morning. Ever."

After the boys went home, I made Arlette go to sleep for a few hours. She kept insisting she wasn't tired, and began a long speech on the relationship of the American antiwar movement and the MNQ. I don't think any such relationship really existed, but Québec terrorists are apt to fall into temporary alliances with a great variety of types. A couple of years ago some of them joined a Black Nationalist plot to dynamite the Statue of Liberty, which was a gift from France, actually, so I suppose it wasn't surprising that Arlette had managed to theorize a common bond with the boys. As with most of her alliances, she had sealed the bond in her cozy little bed, loving them either in turn or in tandem; she had not made that clear, and I did not ask, hoping I would never have to know.

All of that, she had assured me, was over and done with. She was capable of loving only one man at a time, and I was her man now, and the past was the past, and, after all, she had already told me she was no maid, either of Orleans or of Montreal. So I couldn't hold it against her, but neither could I just then develop any tremendous wave of personal enthusiasm for her, so I let her lie in bed by herself instead of keeping her closer company.

She went on talking, and then she stopped abruptly in the middle of a sentence, stopped talking without even reaching a comma, and promptly commenced snoring or breathing heavily, as you prefer. I put in twenty minutes on my back on the floor, relaxing. This wasn't really necessary; I was so relaxed I was afraid my bones would melt.

But it was something to pass the time.

I passed more time drinking coffee and reading and thinking things out. Somewhere to the east of us the Expo began concluding its business for another day. I tried to figure out what the Cubans were doing with the eight or ten people they stole every day. Or more—according to Randy and Seth, that many had disappeared in a matter of hours. But at a rate of ten a day, they would be making off with three hundred victims a month, or something like two thousand in the course of the fair.

Who on earth were they? And what would the Cubans do with them? Where would they even *store* them, for the love of God?

I let Arlette sleep. And, off to the east, I let the fair get ready for sleep itself. As far as I could tell, things got extremely quiet after midnight and ran out of steam entirely by two in the morning, when the entertainment area in La Ronde closed down. There was almost certainly a skeleton crew handling cleanup operations during the dark hours, but it stood to reason that they would be few and far between.

So at two thirty I woke Arlette, who was just as bad at getting up in the middle of the night as at a more reasonable hour. But I poured coffee into her and pointed her at the bathroom, and when she emerged from it, she was alive again.

It was the time for it, certainly. And we had worked out the details reasonably well. She packed a lunch for us in the same paper bag that had contained smoked meat sandwiches a few hours earlier, and I tucked a screwdriver and a chisel and some hunks of plastic into the bag, and away we went.

The weather cooperated. Clouds neatly obscured moon and stars. The streets were virtually deserted. Arlette's car, a Renault *(naturellement)* was in a garage around the block. She fetched it and picked me up and off we went.

The secret of Minna's disappearance, and perhaps Minna herself, were locked in the Cuban Pavilion.

It was time to open the locks.

10

The flashlight worries me," Arlette said. "We are coming closer now. It would not do to be seen."

"A boat without a light would be even more conspicuous."

"Perhaps."

"And wildly unsafe," I added. "When we cut the engines, then we can try running without a light. But not now."

I piloted our little ship down one of the St. Lawrence channels, hopefully in the direction of Île de Nôtre Dame. Arlette crouched in the stern, playing the flashlight over my shoulder at the water ahead of us. The cloud cover had not blown away. The night remained quite black, with only the lights of downtown Montreal shining behind us.

The boat was what we needed and little more, a flat-bottomed rowboat equipped with a small outboard motor. There were a pair of oars as well, and I was glad for them; the motor didn't make all that much noise, but sounds carry on water and I wanted the last leg of our approach to be reasonably silent.

Arlette had arranged for the boat with a simple telephone

call to an unspecified friend. It had been left for us, and we hoped to return it to the same spot where we had found it. Without it we might have had a difficult time; none of the conventional modes of transport at the fair operated at this hour, and, while there were roads and bridges, we could not have used them inconspicuously.

We moved onward, until I could see the shapes of the pavilions not too far in the distance. There was some light there as well but not very much. I cut the engine and told Arlette to put out the flashlight. She asked if she ought to get rid of her cigarette as well. That sounded a little melodramatic to me, but I felt there was no sense crushing the poor girl's sense of theater. I told her we wanted a complete blackout, and she arced the cigarette over the side and into the river.

We moved more slowly with the oars, but it wasn't too bad; the current, such as it was, was on our side. And, wonder of wonders, I did not get lost at all. I guided us neatly from this channel to that channel, placed the blades of the oars smoothly in the water to avoid splashing, and got us right where I wanted to. I didn't have the official Expo map along, which is, no doubt, how I avoided getting lost.

We docked. I tied the painter to a concrete pillar, hauled the oars inside, and stood up on the seat in the middle (which has probably a good nautical name, but it's enough of an accomplishment for me to know about painters and oars and sterns) for a look around. I couldn't see or hear anyone. I hauled myself up onto the shore—it's hard to think of it as a shore when it's paved with asphalt—then leaned down to take the flashlight and the bagful of goodies from Arlette. I helped her up and out, and we hurried through the suddenly deserted streets toward the Cuban Pavilion. For once the more popular pavilions had no line. I was tempted to break into all of them just to see the show.

There was enough light from the streetlamps scattered here and there to make our way, and not enough to show us up readily. In the stillness some sounds of human activity were audible. Motorized sweepers moved through the streets; garbage collectors prepared the concrete bins for tomorrow's assault.

The front entrance to the Cuban Pavilion was too exposed. We slipped around to the back, and I winked the flashlight at the door, then closed in on it and attacked the lock with the tools I had brought. A strip of plastic finally did the trick. I slipped the catch, then had Arlette hold the hunk of plastic in place so that the lock stayed back while I drew the door open. It opened outward, and there was no handle on the outside, so I had to grip the edge of it with my fingertips and sort of coax it open. It took a while, but we managed it and got inside.

I was absolutely certain somebody would grab us the minute we entered. The events in Emile's basement came vividly to mind. I expected a blow on the head, or a gun barrel poked between my ribs, or a bright light flashed in our faces. None of these fears materialized. We stood together in utter silence for almost a full minute, then moved away from the door. I played the beam of the flashlight around the interior of the building. No human forms lurked in the stillness, none but our own.

"We have to be absolutely silent," I whispered. "If

they're kidnapping people, they have to be keeping them somewhere, and they have to have guards. There must be a room here, somewhere. So they must have had the whole thing in mind when they built the damned place, which means they had plenty of time to design something very well hidden."

"Then where do we look?"

"I don't really know. Shhh!"

We wandered around foggily on little cat feet. It was one of the easiest buildings in the world to search—large, empty areaways, no thick inside walls—and one of the hardest in which to find anything. We covered the first floor, climbed the stairs, checked out the second floor, descended the stairs again, and stood around stupidly looking at each other.

"Evan?"

"What?"

"Perhaps the restaurant . . ."

The restaurant was in a separate building. I thought for a moment, then shook my head. "No. More people entered this building than left it. That means they have to be here."

"But where? There is no place to conceal a secret room. The entire roof is a skylight, the walls—"

"Oh, hell," I said. "Of course."

"What?"

"The basement."

"There is a basement? I did not—"

"I didn't either, but there *has* to be a basement. When all of the impossibilities are eliminated, only the possible is left. Or something like that." I was whispering too loudly, and stopped myself. "A hidden basement. It would be no problem to build in something like that. If we look for a seam in the floor—"

"Look at the floor, Evan."

I did, and abandoned that whole train of thought. The floor was tile, and there were seams every ten inches, one as likely as the next to mask the aperture to the cellar below. We checked the entire floor out anyway, just to make sure, and it was no go.

"Then there's a switch that opens it," I went on. "A button, a switch, some way of getting the thing open."

"Reasonable."

"So we must find that switch."

We looked. We went over the whole place, working feverishly now, and all we managed to prove was the invalidity of the hypothesis—there was not a switch. Unless, of course, it lurked behind a secret panel, or was contained in some portable remote-control device.

Or, for that matter, unless it was in the basement. Suppose, when they wanted to open the thing, they signaled their man downstairs, and *he* pressed a button or threw a switch.

It was possible.

Almost anything was possible.

"It's no damned use," I said. "We've checked everywhere."

"It is so. There are only those silly light switches at the entrance, and—"

I hit myself, hard, in the forehead. Arlette looked curiously at me. I tightened my fist and hit myself again in the same spot.

"Oh," she said, light dawning. "It is one of those, then."

"It would have to be."

"But which one?"

We walked to the bank of switches alongside the desk where robot tourists had their Expo Passports stamped. There were seven switches in all. There were also two sets of lights upstairs, three sets downstairs, an air-conditioner—and, if I was right, an electrically-opened passageway to the basement below.

But which one?

I switched off our own flashlight. It didn't' help to stare at the seven switches. They were unlabeled, and one looked rather like the next. And I did not care for the idea of throwing all seven to see what happened, or even of flicking them on one at a time. I did not want to illuminate the pavilion. It was about the last thing I wanted to do.

"She could be down there right now," Arlette whispered. "And we—"

"And we can't get there."

"Oh, it is not fair."

I thought fleetingly of trying to find a way to unscrew all of the bulbs from all of the fixtures. But even that, impossible though it was, would not turn the trick. For all I knew, one of the switches might activate the little recorder that boomed out Castro's speeches, or the Mickey Mouse display unit that told about all of the revolutions throughout the world in the past five million years.

"What do we do?"

"Well," I said, "I guess."

"You guess what?"

"I just guess. I throw a switch and we see what happens."

"Now?"

"Unless you'd like to pray first."

She nodded seriously. "An excellent idea." She knelt and whispered an urgent Paternoster and got to her feet. "Thank you for reminding me, Evan."

St. Joan and the Hidden Basement. I took a breath, and I reached for the board, and I threw a switch. There was just the briefest flicker of light upstairs before I managed to throw the switch down again.

Arlette drew in breath sharply. Her nails dug into my arms. "Do you think—"

"Someone may have noticed, yes. But they won't know where the light came from, or why, and they won't pay any attention to it."

"But if you do it again—"

"I'll wait awhile. Give anyone who saw it time to forget it."

And I did, and tried the second switch, and it was the fixture on the first floor, and that gave us another five minutes to wait. My third try was a loudspeaker—I'm sure the sound from that did not carry any distance, nor did the brief whirring of the air-conditioner, which was try number four. The fifth thing was some more first floor lighting.

"We are getting close," Arlette said.

That was the bright way of looking at it. My own feeling, with five out of seven of the switches exhausted, was that we had leaped to another wrong conclusion—either there was no basement, or none of the damned switches would give us access to it. Well, two more tries would show one way or the other. I pulled the sixth switch and another damned light went on, and I switched it off, and Arlette and I stared at each other in the darkness.

"I don't think your prayers were answered."

"One cannot expect miracles, Evan."

She stood close to me, her head nestled against my shoulder, clutching the paper bag in one hand and the flashlight in the other. I put an arm possessively around her, and I rested the index finger of my free hand upon the sole remaining switch.

"Maybe you ought to pray again," I suggested.

"Oh, Evan—"

"Away we go," I said, and pressed the switch.

And the floor opened up under us.

It was not at all like Alice going down the rabbit hole. Alice, you may remember, seemed to be eternally falling, thinking like mad all the way down. This was nothing like that. One moment I was standing there, joking in the face of adversity like an English soldier in a war movie, and an instant later I was flat on my ass in the darkness. None of that *down down down went Alice*. Just an instantaneous transference from frying pan to fire.

The truly amazing thing, now that I think about it, is how utterly noiseless the whole business was. They must have oiled the mechanism that opened the floor at least a dozen times a day. It opened silently, and we fell silently. And the floor was cushioned, perhaps to prevent harm to whoever got bounced down there during the day, as there were no stairs for anyone to descend. So we landed on the cushioned floor after falling through the easy-opening aperture, and we fell in silence and landed in silence and sat there in silence. I didn't make any noise because I didn't really think of it. Arlette might have screamed, or cried, or moaned or gasped or shrieked, but she didn't. She had fainted, a reaction every bit as dramatic as the others but infinitely safer.

Of course at first I didn't realize she had fainted. At first I thought she had died, and I fumbled around for the flashlight and tried to examine her with it, but it was a casualty of the fall. *She* wasn't, however, as I found out by taking hold of her wrist, where a pulse gently pounded.

I sat there for a moment, trying to think. Then I located the paper bag and pawed through it. Arlette's cigarettes were there, in a clear plastic case, and tucked alongside the blue and white pack was a folder of matches. I scratched one and examined our dungeon.

Which is precisely what it was.

It was deserted, of course. Otherwise we would have been in rather desperate trouble. But, populated or not, the purpose of the subterranean room was instantly obvious. There were no lights about, just unlit candle stubs. There was only one chair, placed there undoubtedly for the convenience of the guard. There were walls and a floor and a ceiling, and everything was dark and bare, and the walls were dotted with chains.

Yes, chains. Chains that hung from the walls, with heavy iron manacles at their ends. Manacles to hold the hands and the feet of prisoners.

It was a setting for a sadomasochist film on the evils of the Spanish Inquisition. It was a stage that cried for whips and rods and fiery tongs, for naked maidens writhing and shrieking, for masked villains flogging them joyously to death. I had done nothing but throw a simple switch, and here I was in the apartment of the Marquis de Sade.

The match warmed my fingertips. I shook it out and lit another one. Beside me Arlette stirred and opened her eyes.

A hideous gurgle found its way forth from her throat. "We have died," she said.

"Arlette—"

"This is hell."

"Arlette."

"We died without a priest, and we are here, and this is hell."

"You're right on the last point," I said. "But we aren't dead. Not yet, at least. This is the basement of the Cuban Pavilion."

"You are lying to me."

"No, I am not. I—"

"We are dead."

"Damn it, we're not!"

"This is hell."

"Not literally."

She was on her feet now, moving inanely around the horrible room. The match went out and she cried out at the sudden darkness. I lit another match and walked alongside her, and she took hold of a pair of manacles and gasped.

"To restrain prisoners, " I explained. "They use them to—"

"The tortures of hell," she said, stepping back.

"No."

"Whips and chains," she said, removing her blouse.

"Arlette—"

"Horrible struggles. Pain," she said, wriggling out of her slacks.

"Good grief—"

"Agony," she moaned, kicking off shoes, squirming out of pants. "Agony, agony, cherished one, darling, agony, agony, take me!"

Some Jeanne d'Arc.

"It was not hell after all," I heard her say.

"I tried to tell you."

"Just now it was rather like heaven." She stretched and sighed. "I must say that I am sorry, Evan. I do not know what came over me."

"I think I did."

"But yes."

I used one of her matches to light her cigarette, then cupped my hand around it and carried it over to light a candle. The glow illuminated most of the dungeon without carrying to the opening in the ceiling.

"This room," she said, thoughtfully. "It is horrid. Also, it excites me."

"I noticed."

"So bold, so——"

"Like tigers," I suggested.

"But of course!" She seized my arm. "You understand, do you not? Precisely like tigers."

"He who rides the tiger," I said, "Must pay the piper."

"Pardon?"

"An old saying, but I seem to have gotten it wrong." I began to recite the limerick about the young lady from Niger, but it didn't work at all well in French. I explained that it was about a young lady who rode upon and subsequently nourished a tiger.

"To be eaten by a tiger," Arlette said. There was an odd

light in her eyes. "To be eaten by—"

I felt it was time to change the subject.

"They must empty the place every night," I said. "They fill it up during the day with whoever they intend to kidnap, and then after the fair closes down, they take them all away somewhere."

"Where?"

"I do not know. Minna was here, Arlette. Right in this crazy room. If I could have found this place sooner—"

"How, Evan?"

"I know. There was no way. They must have moved her out of here the first night. Last night." I turned to look at her. "I don't understand it," I said. "Nobody can kidnap a dozen people a day and still manage to keep the whole operation secret. People don't vanish that way, not without making waves. I just don't get it."

"What shall we do now?"

"I don't know."

"If we stay here—"

"No." I went over to her and took a sandwich from the paper bag. I sat down and gnawed at it but couldn't develop enough of an appetite to finish it. I wrapped it again in waxed paper and returned it to the bag. Arlette took a last drag from her cigarette, stubbed it out on the heel of her shoe, and put it in the paper bag along with our sandwiches and burglar tools.

"Perhaps I could conceal myself here," Arlette suggested.

"How?"

"I do not know. It is so bare, so desolate. Perhaps you could shackle me to the wall and leave me, and when they return in a few hours, they will think I was left behind by error."

"I don't think that would work."

"Nor do I. Nevertheless . . ."

I tried to think it through on my own. Minna, along with any number of other persons, had been confined to the basement dungeon. She was not here now. Thus, I reasoned, either she and her fellow prisoners had been removed to other quarters, or else their captors had—

I didn't want to think about it. It was inconceivable, I told myself, that the Cubans would have murdered them all. But it was equally inconceivable that Minna could have been kidnapped in the first place. I got up and paced the floor, back and forth and back and forth, pushing things around in my mind in an attempt to force them into some sort of order.

"Evan, it is late."

"I know."

"If we do not leave soon—"

"I know."

"For soon the dawn will break, and without the cover of darkness—"

"Dammit, I *know*."

We could try keeping them under surveillance, I thought. Seth and Randy would cooperate. We could post a guard around the pavilion and see what happened tomorrow night when the crowds left.

Better yet, I thought, we could bug the place. The MNQ might be composed of a bunch of half-mad fanatics, but there was considerable technological ability to draw upon. It shouldn't be too difficult to return to the dungeon and plant a microphone or two in the walls. If nothing else, that would clear up some of the mystery surrounding the whole affair. If we could overhear what went on inside the dungeon during the day, when it was packed to capacity with prisoners and guards, we would at least have some sort of idea what we were up against.

In the meantime, though, there was next to nothing to do. "Evan—"

"You're right," I said. "We have to get out of here."

"If anything were to be gained by staying—"

"No, you're right," I said. "Let's go."

We tried to clean up all traces of our visit. We added the broken flashlight to the collection of useless articles in the paper bag and tossed it carefully through the aperture to the floor above. I blew out the candle as soon as I had collected all of the burnt matches from the floor. Then we moved to directly below the opening, and I crouched down so that Arlette could climb onto my shoulders. I straightened up, and she got her arms over the edge and pulled herself through.

There were a few bad moments during which it seemed as though I would have to stay in the dungeon forever. I couldn't quite jump high enough to get a purchase on the rim of the aperture, and I knew that Arlette was not strong enough to haul me up. I kept jumping and not quite making it, and Arlette was becoming quietly hysterical.

Ultimately I dragged over the single chair and stood on it. I jumped again, and caught the rim but couldn't hold onto it, and came down heavily to the left of the chair. I tried again, and this time I caught hold of the rim and didn't let go. Arlette gave me what help she could. I started slipping at the last minute, but then I managed to get one leg up and sort of spilled myself out onto the tiled floor. I didn't move at first, and Arlette asked me if I was all right, and I said I was.

"How do the Cubans get out, Evan?"

I said I didn't know. Perhaps they lowered a rope ladder, or perhaps they used a step stool and dragged it up after them. "It doesn't matter," I told her. "We'll come back tomorrow night and plant a couple of microphones. I'm sure someone from the movement will be able to help us—"

"Claude, if he will help. Or others."

"Good." I took a deep breath and let it out slowly. "At least we know the physical plant here. We won't be working blind anymore." I looked at my watch. "We were down there too long. We'd better get the hell out of here."

"The chair, Evan. Will they not notice it?"

"Perhaps."

"Is there no way to return it to its place?"

"None I can think of. Maybe they'll ignore it. The hell with it."

"I could go down and return it, and then you could try to pull me out, and—"

"And then we'd be back where we started from."

"Yes."

We got ready to go, and I threw the switch to close the aperture in the floor. It slid shut as silently as it had opened. Once it was closed, I dropped to my hands and knees to try to locate the seams in the floor. Even now, knowing where it was, I couldn't distinguish any seams. The trapdoor was superbly engineered.

But why go to the trouble?

"Come on," I said, taking Arlette's hand. "I realize it's hard for you to tear yourself away from such an enchanting place—"

"It is evil here. Satanic."

We didn't have to jimmy the door this time. The lock served only to keep people out. The door swung open easily, and I stuck my head out and looked and listened. I heard a car approaching and drew back inside. The car passed perhaps a hundred feet from us and kept on going. We waited until the sound of the engine died in the distance. Then I stuck my head out again, and looked and listened again, and the coast was as clear as it seemed likely to get. We slipped out in to the night and headed for our boat. I held the paper bag in one hand and Arlette's hand in the other. We walked quickly, less frightened of shadows now, less worried about the possibility of discovery.

Where would they take the prisoners? I thought it over and decided that the answer depended upon the motive. If they wanted ransom, for example, there would be no particular point in spiriting them out of the country; they would do better to keep them on some hidden estate in the Canadian countryside. If, on the other hand, they had some other use planned for them, they might want to get them out of Canada and into Cuba as quickly as possible.

The second line of reasoning seemed more logical. You couldn't attempt to ransom a wholesale lot of prisoners without attracting attention. For that matter, you couldn't invest that kind of money in a kidnapping for financial gain. The costs of building the pavilion, the costs of the entire arrangement—

Of course they might intend a wholesale exchange, I thought. They had traded prisoners for drugs once before, hadn't they? And maybe the ransom demands would be directed against the United States Government. "If you want the victims back, vacate Guantanamo Bay"—something like that.

I got fairly involved with thoughts like this. I held Arlette's hand and hurried her along. And, because we had already been to the Cuban Pavilion and had left it undiscovered, I didn't really worry much about someone spotting us.

I suppose the same thing happens to cat burglars and others of that ilk. Creep about long enough in silence and in darkness, and eventually one becomes sufficiently comfortable in that environment to dispense with fear. This happened to us. All we had to do was get to the boat and go home, and that's what we were going to do. As far as I was concerned, the party was over.

My mistake.

I saw the man, perhaps a hundred yards ahead of us on the right. He was running toward us, and I grabbed Arlette and slapped a hand over her mouth to keep her from crying out. We dropped down to the ground at the side of the path.

Then the man stopped, abruptly. Forms had materialized out of the shadows, three of them. Someone cried out, but I could not make out what was said.

"Evan—"

"*Shhh!*"

Something metallic glinted in the darkness. There was a sudden movement, and then a crisp volley of shots rang out, and the man who had been running let out a brief cry and clutched himself. Then, in slow motion, he crumpled up and fell gently to the ground.

More movement. A man rushed to him, dropped to the ground, picked something up, straightened up and ran. Two other men were with him. Together they bolted from the man who had been shot and tore up the path toward us. I held onto Arlette and kept her close beside me in the darkness. The trio of assassins passed within a few yards of us without stopping. They ran on down on the path behind us, and we stayed absolutely motionless until their footsteps had disappeared in the night.

When the sound of footfalls ceased, Arlette started to move. I stopped her with a hand on her shoulder and held my finger to her lips. She subsided. For five hourlike minutes we remained where we were, silent, still. I waited for the sound of a siren, waited for one of the wandering guards to happen on the scene. The sounds of the gunshots had been extraordinarily loud in the silence of the night, and it seemed impossible that no one would come.

If someone did, I didn't want to be moving around.

But no one came. I looked at my watch and decided that no one was going to come now. I stood up, and Arlette rose to her feet beside me.

She said, "Who was—"

"I don't know. Let's find out."

The man, tall and thin and dark and dead, lay sprawled in the middle of the carpet of plastic grass fronting the Man In The Home Pavilion. He had bled all over that artificial lawn, and soon the world would discover if it was in fact as wondrously washable as its promoters claimed. I went through the formality of looking for a pulse. There was none.

I patted his pockets, found nothing. I picked up the murder gun from the grass beside his body, sniffed the barrel, threw it down again. I wondered if the dead man was a Cuban—he did not look particularly Cuban—or if he had been killed by Cuban agents. I wondered how he fit into everything, if at all.

"Do you know him, Evan?"

"No."

"Who killed him?"

"I don't know that either." I was suddenly dizzy, and took deep breaths to steady myself. We were in over our heads, I thought. We were playing a fool's game with people who knew the rules far better than we.

"I think we should get out of here," I said.

"I agree."

This time we walked onward with caution. This time we moved in absolute silence, our ears attuned to the night sounds around us. This time, as we walked down the path to the waterway, we did not make the mistake of assuming we were alone.

But we still weren't quite prepared. We reached the water's edge, and I saw our little boat right where we had left it. And, alongside it, I saw another large boat, empty.

Arlette's hand tightened on my arm. And from the shadows a man emerged. There was a gun in his hand. He was smiling slightly, and he went on smiling as he placed the muzzle of the gun within three inches of my chest, directly over the heart.

Then he said, in highly accented French, "The bullet that will kill me is not yet cast."

11

T

he bullet that will kill me is not yet cast.

How interesting, I thought. It was a claim I myself would have liked to make, but one that if made would soon prove to be demonstrably false. Because I had the unassailable feeling that the bullet that would kill me *had* been cast, and that it reposed at that very moment in the cylinder of the revolver that was pointing at my heart.

"The bullet that will kill me is not yet cast," the man repeated, a touch of malice in his voice. I looked at the gun and tried to estimate my chances against it. I could make some sort of grab for it, try to knock it aside and beat the idiot's brains out. I readied myself, and then I took careful note of the way the index finger was curled tautly around the trigger. He wasn't just pointing the gun at me. He was getting ready to fire it.

"Nor is the bullet yet cast, nor shall it ever be cast, that can put to death a grand idea. Nor is the bullet cast that will slay France."

The same accent, the same vaguely familiar yet quietly meaningless sort of rhetoric. But the speaker was not the man now. It was Arlette, her voice ringing with conviction, her hand still firm in its grip upon my arm.

"And so I pledge myself," she went on, "and my honor, and my life and soul, to the overthrow of the Bourbon yoke and the prompt restoration of the seed of empire—"

"Enough," the man was saying now. "Enough, more than enough." He lowered the gun and pocketed it. "You will understand that I have little use for such passwords as you yourself, but at such times one cannot do less than display maximum caution." He smiled savagely. "Of course I heard the shots. I was on the water when they sounded, and made my approach in silence. How was I to know who triumphed, eh? You could have been dead, and your assailants after me. Eh?"

"Of course."

"You have the money?"

"Yes," I said, wondering idly what money he meant, and who he was, and what Arlette had said to him, and what, for that matter, we were all of us doing here. "Yes," I said. "I have it."

"Very good. You will want this, of course."

He handed me a flat black attaché case. I took it by the handle and ran my hand over the side of it. Fine leather, soft, smooth.

"And I will want—the paper sack? Yes?"

"But certainly," I said, and handled him our sandwiches and burglar tools.

He patted it lovingly, then turned from us and tossed the sack into his own boat. He turned to face us again. "You might tell the man that we can undertake to ship more frequently if the market position holds up. You will tell him that?"

"Certainly."

"I myself am only a courier. I speak messages as they are given to me, just as I relay parcels as I receive them. No offense?"

"None at all."

"I am glad," he said. He smiled again, like a wolf baring

its teeth, vaulted into his boat, and turned a key in the ignition. His engines roared into life and his boat dashed off to the east.

Without a word, Arlette and I got into our own little boat. I bent over the little outboard motor and cranked it.

"The sound of the engine," she began.

"The hell with it," I said. "I want to get out of here in a hurry."

The engine caught. I spun the boat around and headed back in the direction from which we had come; the opposite direction the large vessel had taken. I wanted to get as far away from him as possible. I did not ever want to see that man again.

"Evan?"

"Yes?"

"This satchel."

"Yes?"

"Do you know what is in it?"

"No."

"Neither do I. Why did he take our sandwiches?"

"Perhaps he was hungry."

She lapsed into a hurt silence. I piloted our little boat through the dark waters. Everything had gone quietly mad. I felt as though we were playing out parts in a script based upon a painting by Salvador Dali. Who was the dead man? Who killed him and why? Where did the other man come from, and why had he given us the satchel, and what was he talking about, babbling that the bullet that would kill him had not been cast? And Arlette—

"You knew the answer," I said suddenly.

"Pardon?"

"You knew the rest of the password."

"What password?"

"The bullet that would kill him."

"Evan, are you feeling well?"

"No," I said, "but that has nothing to do with it. Look, he pointed a gun at us. At me, actually. And he said something about a bullet—"

" 'The bullet that will kill me is not yet cast.' "

"Right."

"Was that a password?"

"It seems so. And you answered him. Didn't you know it was a password?"

"But no."

"Then how in hell—"

"It was a saying of Napoleon," she said.

I thought for a moment. She was right, I thought—it *was* a saying of Napoleon, uttered in 1814 at Montereau. It was the sort of smart-ass remark military leaders are apt to make, especially when they're sitting in tents a few miles behind the front lines.

So Napoleon said it. Wonderful. And the man with the gun might easily have been nutty enough to think he was Napoleon. But—

"You answered him," I said.

"Yes."

"Are you Josephine or something?"

She frowned. "Evan, you must be very tired. You had no sleep tonight and I doubt that you slept much last night either. As soon as we return to the apartment—"

"You answered him."

"Yes."

"What did you say?"

"I continued the oath."

"The oath?" I looked at her. "What oath?"

"The Bonapartiste oath."

"Oh."

"He seemed to be waiting for an answer, and—"

"Yes, of course."

"So I continued the oath." She hesitated for a moment. "It would perhaps be better if you did not tell the others, but I am a Bonapartiste. I do not believe that it is incompatible with the movement for the liberation of Québec, although there are those who would disagree with me. But should not French Canada and France herself be united under a strong leader, a single leader who is a descendent of the great Napoleon himself and who will again restore French glory and French empire throughout the world and who will—"

"Oh," I said.

"Pardon?"

"That man spoke with an unusual accent."

"Yes."

"A Corsican accent, wasn't it?"

She thought it over. "It is possible. I could not say."

"I think it was. It sounded a little like French spoken by an Italian, didn't it? A Corsican accent."

"Napoleon was a Corsican."

"Yes."

"So the man was a Bonapartiste, Evan. It is simple, no? I did not think the Cause had much activity in this hemisphere, but—"

I shook my head. "I do not think the man was a Bonapartiste."

"But of course! You yourself said he was a Corsican, and he recited the oath, the beginning of the oath—"

"I think he used the oath as a password. A fairly natural password for a Corsican, I guess."

"Then—"

"A Corsican coming to Montreal to exchange a parcel for some money."

"But we gave him sandwiches and tools," she said. "And my cigarettes. Damn, I want a cigarette!"

"You'll have to wait. He didn't know we gave him sandwiches and tools. He thought we gave him money."

"I see."

I don't know whether she did or not, but I did. The Corsican had come to meet someone, someone who was carrying a consignment of cash. The man with the money was ambushed and shot, and he had left his blood all over the plastic lawn at the Man In The Home Pavilion. His murderers took the cash, and Arlette and I went on to meet the Corsican.

And gave him lunch. And took, in return, what?

I had a fair idea.

They grow it in Turkey, in huge fields where the workers earn fifteen or twenty cents a day. They ship it to France, where the men of the Union Corse, the Corsican Mafia, refine it carefully in hidden laboratories. Then they ship it to Canada, and there French Canadians buy it and cut it and parcel it out and ship it once more to New York and Philadelphia and Chicago and Detroit.

Uh-huh.

I managed to sail us back to where Arlette's friend had left the boat for us. I tied up the boat, and Arlette and I returned to her apartment. Dawn was breaking by the time we got back. Arlette tore open a pack of Gauloise and lit a cigarette. I sat down on the bed and opened the attaché case, and inside were three cylindrical tins. I managed to open one of them, wet a finger, dipped it into the white powder, and licked it.

Uh-huh.

"What is it, Evan?"

I capped the tin, returned it to the case. I sat with the case open on my lap and looked down at the three tins. The Union Corse was not going to be happy about this, I thought. Neither, for that matter, were the men who were supposed to be on the receiving end of the shipment. Nor the ultimate consumers, who would start walking up the walls when the supply ran thin.

"Evan?"

"It's heroin," I said quietly. "Three kilos of it, I guess. Enough heroin to turn on half the world."

She had dozens of questions. She wanted to know why we had it and whose it was and what I proposed to do with it. I couldn't answer the last question and didn't have the strength to answer the others. I just sat there and looked at the three tins and thought about Mounties and Cubans and French Canadians and Corsicans and wondered, without particularly caring, which of them would kill me first.

Arlette finished her cigarette, then got undressed and into bed. She was quite surprised, and perhaps a little bit hurt, when I did not want to make love. She found it difficult to understand. I sat with her until she fell asleep, and then I found the brandy bottle and communed with it until it was empty.

The sun came up, hot as ever. I prowled through Arlette's cupboards until I found an old bottle of cooking sherry, and I drank that, too. On the seven o'clock newscast I learned that a body had been discovered at the Expo site, and that foul play was feared. At eight o'clock I discovered that De Gaulle had made a forceful speech at Lyon, coming out foursquare for the independence of Québec. At eight thirty Arlette's radio assured me that a spokesman for Mrs. Battenberg had denied that Free Québec sentiment would affect plans for a royal visit to the fair.

At nine o'clock fingerprints on the murder gun were positively identified as belonging to Evan Michael Tanner, American, fugitive from justice, kidnapper, terrorist, and killer.

I looked at the heroin and wished I had a hypodermic needle.

12

"Of course you realize that it is suicide."

"I know this," Emile said.

"Utter suicide. You would not have a chance."

"I do not expect a chance. I am not a fool, Evan."

I doubted this. I looked at Emile, then glanced at the bed where Arlette was still sleeping. It was somewhere around noon and she was still asleep and I envied her. Insomnia, I decided, was more curse than blessing. Arlette managed to escape the slipstream of human madness for eight hours out of every twenty-four. God, how I envied her.

I looked again at Emile. He was seated, with Jean and Jacques Berton crouching at his right like couchant lions while Claude hulked grimly at his left. He didn't *look* mad, I thought. And when he spoke, he seemed quite calm and rational. Until one happened to pay attention to his words.

"I am not afraid to die, Evan."

"It is not a question of personal fear. The movement—"

"The movement needs our deaths more than our lives." The sentence has at least a grand a ring to it in French as in English. "The movement cries out for martyrs, Evan. The MNQ is—admit it—in many quarters no more than a joke. A majority of those who sympathize with us nevertheless regard us as cranks, as unworldly fanatics. Is it not so?"

"All extremist movements begin in that fashion, Emile—"

"And how is public opinion changed?"

I didn't get a chance to answer that one. "By fire and blood," Claude cut in. He coughed and spat for emphasis. "By the grand act, by sacrifice."

"Exactly," said Emile. "Exactly. The grand act, bold and daring and dramatic. The act need not be logical. It may be senseless, it may be foredoomed to failure. This does not matter. But it must be an act that brings counteraction, an act that yields a crop of martyrs for the cause. The soil of liberty is fertilized by the blood of martyrs. You know this is true, Evan. You know full well that nothing rallies the public to a cause like the demonstrated willingness of patriots to die for it."

I might have argued more forcefully if I hadn't happened to know that he was absolutely correct. My mind could do nothing more than summon up examples that proved his point. The 1916 Easter Rebellion in Dublin took place with half the country opposed to republicanism and the other half profoundly apathetic. The rising was squashed, as its leaders knew it would be; the British executed the leaders, as everyone had assumed they would—and two years later Sinn Féin swept the national elections in a landslide.

The situation in Québec was much further from fulfillment, of course. But the basic pattern remained the same. Martyrs, sacrificing themselves heroically for an ideal, would do more than reams of propaganda to change the Québec nationalists from a laughingstock to a political force.

I closed my eyes. Claude was talking. On the bed Arlette moaned in her sleep; perhaps his rough voice was giving her bad dreams. I myself was not paying any attention to what he was saying. If Emile was right (and I had to admit that he was) and if I truly supported the cause of the MNQ (and I certainly did), then I ought to be backing him and Claude and the Berton Boys all the way.

But I wasn't.

Because they had decided, all of them, that they were going to abandon the kidnapping plans entirely. And they had decided, all of them, that they were going to put into effect the public assassination of the Queen of England.

And no matter how I looked at it, this just didn't seem like a good idea.

"I don't understand one thing," I cut in. "Yesterday you opposed assassination, Emile. Yesterday you said—"

"Yesterday was a thousand years ago."

It seemed that way to me, all right. "But what has changed your mind?"

"You heard the General's speech? You heard the words of the grand Charles?"

"I caught a newscast, yes. But—"

"You must hear the entire speech, Evan. Then perhaps you will realize what has changed my mind, as you put it." He smiled gently at me, a wise old teacher being patient with a slow but willing pupil. "The General is very highly respected throughout French Canada, Evan. By publicly endorsing our cause, he has advanced the timetable of rebellion by years. Years! It is not merely that he has focused attention upon us. He has done more than this. He has lent us the support of his worldwide prestige. He has told the world that the cause of Québec is the cause of France. Yesterday it would have been good strategy to kidnap the Queen. It would have generated publicity that we were greatly in need of. Today all has changed. Our position is stronger, Evan, and our needs are different."

"It has always been that way. The bitch must die." This from Claude.

"Let us not quarrel." Emile spread his hands. "To kidnap the Queen now would merely draw everyone's sympathy to her. Is it not so, Evan? The public identifies with those who suffer. The long, drawn-out suffering, the man trapped in a cave-in, the child in a well, the kidnapped baby—everyone sheds tears for them. So it would be with her."

"People sort of sympathize with victims of assassination, too."

"It is not the same. Then the act is quick, terrible, perhaps brutal, but it is over. And the martyrdom of the Queen—innocent, yes, but who is not innocent?—her martyrdom blends with and is overshadowed by our own. The crowd seizes us, we are torn to pieces, our names are on the lips of the multitude. The Queen becomes, not our victim, but the victim of history—"

"The bitch must die." Claude again.

"And we must die with her. You talk, Evan, of my personal value to the movement. It is true that I have been something of an organizer. But I am old, you know, and my value in this respect is approaching its end. The future belongs to youth, and it is they who will continue my organizational work. My supreme value will lie in martyrdom."

"So you'll be in on the killing?"

"Yes. And Claude, and both Jean and Jacques. Just we four."

"I see."

He lowered his eyes. "I had intended to invite you to join us, Evan, but I was voted down. And the others, I suspect, are correct, your own devotion notwithstanding. They felt that as an American citizen, as someone neither French nor Canadian, it would not do to have you publicly identified with the act of assassination. I hope you will not feel slighted . . ."

Not in the least, I thought.

"We know your work is important to us, and it will continue to aid our cause in years to come." The gentle smile again. "Of course you must envy those of us who are privileged to die as heroes. But in a way you too are to be envied. For it is you, Evan, who will see the fruits of what we begin. While we, like Moses, lead our children to the gates of the Promised Land, you, like Joshua, will actually enter the vineyards of Canaan."

"So we'll enter the vineyards of Canaan," I told Arlette. "You and me, cherished one, and the grapes of wrath. And to think you slept through it all."

"I wish I had been awake."

"I wish I hadn't."

"But why? You regret that you may not join them?" Her eyes searched mine and she frowned slightly. "Evan, is it that you do not approve of the assassination?"

"It is just that."

"You think it is unwise? But why?"

I got up and walked around. "Because it's harebrained," I said. "Because it's misplaced violence, because it's stupid, because it's dangerous, because it's moronic—"

"You feel it will hurt the cause?"

"It will exterminate the cause. I just don't understand Emile. He's got the wrong slant entirely on the way public opinion operates. He and the rest of them expect to die, but that won't be the end of it. Twenty-four hours after the Queen dies, every member of the MNQ will be in jail. All of the other separatist groups will be rounded up. I don't suppose there will be a war—"

"A war!"

"It's not impossible, but I'd tend to rule it out. France and Canada will probably break off diplomatic relations. France and England will almost certainly do so—they haven't been getting along well anyway, and this should do it once and for all. France may have a revolution. Québec will be pure hell for a long time, and in the other provinces French Canadians won't have it very easy. A batch of peasants will get beaten to death." I sighed. "Maybe the world will come to an end. That will clear up all the problems, at least, and I can't think of any other way out."

"But this is horrible!"

"That's the general idea."

"But we must do something!"

"Oh?"

"If it is as bad as you said—"

"It's probably worse than I said. My mind isn't working that well today. I'm not up to imagining just how bad it is."

"Then we must act! We must stop them!"

I got some coffee and poured the last of the brandy into it. I thought of the planning session Emile and Claude and the Bertons and I had conducted while lucky Arlette had slept. They were all good at conspiracy and their plan was a solid one. Stop them? That was a good idea, all right. But how?

I said, "Would you betray them, Arlette?"

"To be a traitor? Oh, that is a bad thought!"

"We could do that, you see. All we have to do is make a phone call to the authorities. We tell them just what's going to happen and where, and they'll pick up our four heroes before a single chunk of plastique gets detonated. The good lady will be safe and four Québeçois patriots will spend the rest of their lives in prison. And you and I will be traitors."

"We cannot do that."

"I agree. What else can we do?"

She stubbed out a cigarette. She looked up at me, little Joan of Arc, wet-eyed and lost. "I do not know," she said.

"Neither do I. I can't even think straight."

"But we will think, both of us. Of course you cannot put your mind to it, not when you are so worried about Minna. The poor little girl! Those chains, that dungeon—"

"Well, she's not in there now, anyway."

"And we shall discover where she is, Evan. Tonight we shall plant the microphone, as you said. We shall go to the

Cuban place and hide the microphone, and tomorrow we shall go to where the poor little angel is hidden, and we shall free her, and when that is done, we shall be able to find some way to keep the Queen from being killed."

"No."

"No? But why?"

"Because your timetable is a little off," I said. "I guess you missed the best part of all. What time is it?"

"Time?"

"Now. What time is it now?"

"Seventeen minutes after four, but this clock is perhaps two or three minutes slow, so—"

"That's close enough. Four seventeen p.m. Saturday. Which means that we have, let me see, just short of twenty-eight hours—"

"Twenty-eight hours!"

I nodded. "Twenty-eight hours to pull off the whole operation. Because, according to present plans, Mrs. Battenberg is going to be blown to bits at eight tomorrow night. There will be a fireworks display on La Ronde to celebrate the centennial of the Canadian Confederation, and the Queen will sail down the Saint Lawrence to see it, and that's where they're going to get her. Twenty-eight goddamn hours."

I spent one of the twenty-eight hours with a pencil and notebook. I sent Arlette out hunting for some sort of listening device that would enable us to bug the Cuban dungeon, and while she was gone I sat around the apartment making lists.

All of those books that tell you how to make a million

dollars and win friends and manipulate people and become head of your company and be the richest kid on your block, all of those terrible books seem to contain the same little formula for solving problems. When you've got a hundred impossible things to do, what you do is write them all down. Then you number them in order of importance, and then you drop everything and concentrate on problem number one, and you break your neck until it's done, and then you go on to problem number two, and you persevere in this fashion, problem by problem, until you either solve all of your problems or die of a coronary, which actually does tend to wipe the slate clean.

I had made lists of this sort before out of the same general sort of multifaceted desperation. I couldn't remember that they had ever done any demonstrable good, but maybe that was due to my failure to follow through all the way. What usually happened was this—I got everything listed, and I read through the list a few times to see just how many impossible and unpleasant things I had to do, and then I tore up the list and went out and got drunk. Then the next day I would just do whatever I could, in whatever order suggested itself, and in my usual haphazard fashion I would somehow blunder through.

Maybe the present situation demanded closer allegiance to the formula. I wasn't sure. In any case, I opened a notebook and picked up a pencil and wrote *Minna*.

I looked at her name for a while and pondered worlds of unanswerable questions. Where was she? How had she gotten there? What did they intend to do with her?

Then I wrote down *Assassination*. And, on the same line, *Sunday 8 p.m.* Maybe there was a way after all, I thought.

I could tip off the authorities anonymously, and then I could get word to Emile that the authorities knew about it, and he and the others from MNQ would be able to abort the entire operation. If the police were already on the spot—

Of course Claude and the Bertons might be hotheaded enough to try going ahead with it anyway. But at least it would save the Queen and might even keep everybody in the clear. I beamed momentarily; maybe the list-making had something to be said for it after all.

Of course De Gaulle's remark had been a godsend, and of course it *was* time for martyrdom, for the grand act, and if only there were some way short of assassination—

I turned my mind back to my list. I was by no means through with it. On the next line down I wrote *Heroin.*

Now there was another one to conjure with. What the hell was I going to do with the heroin? I didn't even want to think about its value, but it had to be truly enormous. There seemed no question but that the world would be considerably better off if I flushed it all down the toilet, but I wasn't entirely certain that I would be. Even if possession were nine points of the law, the heroin remained one-tenth the property of the Union Corse, and I had the feeling they would consider that tenth the most important part of the equation.

If they knew I had the heroin—and my fingerprints on the damned murder gun would surely put that unpleasant idea in their heads—then they would want it back and would feel unkindly toward me for having it. It is not inordinately wise to have someone like the Union Corse mad at you.

So I would have gladly given it back to them, no questions asked. But how was I to go about doing that? I looked at my list, and I stared myopically at the word *Heroin*, and then I took a breath and moved on to the next line and licked the tip of my pencil and wrote *Cops*.

Because it did look as though I had established myself now and forever as Public Enemy Number One on both sides of the U.S.-Canadian border. The murder charge was the final straw. Sooner or later someone was going to catch me, and when that happened, I didn't know what the hell I was going to do. The Chief might decide to come to my aid, and then again he might not; meanwhile, there was no way for me to get in touch with him. I didn't even know the bastard's name. And even if he did try to help, he would have to fight the police of two countries for me, and I was by no means certain that he swung enough weight. As things stood, I could not remain in Canada, nor could I go back to the States.

I looked at the list, drawing some comfort from the fact that the word *Cops* was at the bottom of it. That meant I wasn't supposed to worry about it for the time being. I was supposed to put it clear out of my mind, along with *Heroin* and *Assassination*. Meanwhile, I would devote one hundred percent of my time and effort to Item One: *Minna*.

Which meant—

Which meant, I decided, that I was precisely back where I had started. If I had made any progress, I was damned if I could see what it was. I had a few words written in a notebook, and I had let the clock go ticking onward, and that was about the size of it. It looked as though I were never going to make a million dollars or win friends or manipulate people or become head of my firm or be the richest kid on my block. Or rescue Minna, or thwart the assassination, or unload the heroin, or clear myself with the police.

This was as far as I had ever gotten with the list-making process. Now, according to the rules, it was time for me to go out and get drunk. I would have liked to, but I didn't dare go out, for one thing, and I couldn't dismiss the feeling that getting drunk right about now might be a bad idea.

And so, on the theory that action is better than inaction, I did the only thing I could think of at the time. I tore up the list.

By the time Arlette came back with the microphone and receiver, our twenty-eight hours were down to twenty-seven. By the time I left her apartment and headed for the Cuban dungeon, they had been further reduced to seventeen. The intervening ten hours were awful.

For openers, Arlette's mood was one of incautious optimism, a mood I found myself wholly incapable of sharing. I suppose she felt better in part because she had gone out and done something while I sat making idiot lists. Whatever the explanation, she was bubbling like a percolator. We had the microphone, therefore we were on the right track, therefore we would save Minna and the Queen and liberate Québec and discover a cure for cancer and live happily ever after.

She wanted to celebrate horizontally.

Well, I didn't.

I'm perfectly aware that this was the wrong attitude for me to take. It wasn't as though I were busy doing something else, because I couldn't do anything until the fair closed for the day. So we certainly had time to make love, and she certainly had the inclination, and I didn't, and that's not the way red-blooded men are supposed to act. James Bond, for example, would have unhesitatingly bounced her into bed the moment she came through the door. He would not even have waited for the triumphal presentation of microphone and receiver. If he had been given to list-making, *Ball Arlette* would have been right up there at the top, and until it was done and done well, he would not even have given a thought to the other dilemmas.

In case you have not yet doped it out, I am not in his league.

Nor, however, am I an utter cad. When Arlette began hinting at the idea of bed, I tried to pretend that I was just too thickheaded to follow her lead. She responded by throwing subtlety to the winds and her clothes to the floor, and I joined her on the bed and kissed her and cuddled her, quietly determined to play out my part properly whether I felt like it or not.

My heart was in the right place, but that was the only thing that was. Arlette did everything she could think of, along with a few things that I don't suppose I could have thought of. She worked desperately to demonstrate her loyalty to French culture, but nothing worked. When she realized that nothing would do any good, she dashed from the bed to the bathroom and stood inside crying her eyes out. The little room must have acted as an echo chamber; I think they could have heard her crying ten miles away.

I tried the door. It was locked. I told her to come out and she announced that she was going to slash her wrists and kill herself. I told her that it was certainly not her fault, and that if anyone deserved slashing it was me, and that I could think of something other than wrists to attack.

When she emerged finally, her pretty face washed free of tears, she came to me and patted my cheek sympathetically. "Jean d'Arc," she said. "My chaste hero, my knight in shiny armor. Your mind is on other things, you burn with devotion to the cause, of course you must not make love to Arlette."

She seemed convinced. I'm not sure I was. I thought of the list of things I couldn't do and realized I had one more thing to add to it. When impotence strikes, it hits you everywhere.

We sat around for a while, waiting for the fair to close up shop, and then it occurred to me to test the microphone and the receiving gadget, and the thing didn't work. Arlette remembered that someone had dropped the mike recently. I took it apart with a screwdriver and found a broken thing in it. I don't know what the broken thing was, or what it was supposed to do. But without it we seemed to be up a tree.

She got us out of that one. She told me she had an idea and left without an explanation. I wasn't sorry to see her go—we'd been getting on each other's nerves—but I didn't really expect her to come up with anything. She did, though, returning with Seth and Randy in tow. Seth handed me a microphone and asked me if it would work.

"I don't know," I said. "Where's the receiver?"

"Probably in police headquarters. It's one of the bugs they put in our office. Somebody fastened it to the underside of the mimeo machine."

"We thought you could rob it of the broken part and repair ours," Arlette said.

"This is a live mike," I said.

Somebody nodded.

"They can pick up what we're saying right now, at police headquarters or wherever."

"Yes, but—"

"Be quiet," I said.

I took the bug apart. It was a completely different model from ours, but it had a piece like the piece that was broken in our unit, and I studied the way it was connected and took it out and put it in our mike. When we tested it again, it worked. I demolished the rest of the draft-dodgers' bug with my shoe. It seemed faintly possible that our mike would now send signals to our receiver and to the police unit as well, but I decided that this was another possibility to be added to the long unwritten list of things that ought not to be thought about.

The next few hours were deadly. The four of us sat around listening to the radio. I kept changing stations to avoid listening to a newscast. They weren't going to tell me anything I wanted to hear.

I finally got out of there. Arlette wanted to come along, perhaps in the hope that the dungeon would once again unlock my libido. Seth and Randy also volunteered to join me. I insisted on going alone. It would be easy this time. I merely had to get into the building, press the switch (I knew which one it was, for a change), hide the bug some-where, close up shop, and leave.

I found the boat and had no trouble following last night's

course to Île de Nôtre Dame. I docked at precisely the same spot. I left the boat and carried the bug with me to the Cuban Pavilion, and then a bad day turned worse.

They had guards posted. Four of them, two in front and two at the rear. Four armed guards who stood rigidly at attention and who gave every appearance of being wholly alert.

For a long time I sat in the shadows and watched them from a distance. They didn't fall asleep or go away or die or anything of the sort. They stayed right where they were and seemed likely to stay there until the fair reopened in the morning.

I went back to my boat and began rowing. I half hoped it would sink, but it didn't. Boats never sink when you want them to.

13

They were all at the apartment when I got back. I knocked on the door and Arlette opened it, and I walked in flipping the microphone up in the air and catching it, flipping and catching, like George Raft's half dollar bit. I ignored their questions and went on playing with the microphone. It was about the size of a plum but less useful.

"Guards all over the place," I explained eventually. "We must have left something behind in the dungeon the other night. I don't know what—a cigarette butt, maybe. Or maybe they always have guards except on Saturdays. That doesn't make much sense, but neither does anything else lately. It doesn't matter. The place is guarded and there's no way to plant the bug and I think I've just about had it. Is there anything to drink?"

"No."

"That's wonderful," I said.

Seth mentioned that there was a little wine back at their place. I told him not to bother. "Or we could turn on," he suggested.

I looked at Arlette. "I thought I told you to keep quiet about that."

"About what, Evan?"

"You holding, Evan?"

"But I said nothing," Arlette said. "I never mentioned the heroin."

"Heroin?" Randy looked carefully at me. "You're no junkie, it can't be that. What's the bit?"

"What did you mean about turning on?"

There's something to be said for answering a question with a question. Randy forgot his and answered mine. "Well," he said, "like pot."

"You have some with you?"

"Well, actually, yes."

I turned to Arlette. "You've been this route, Joan of Arc?"

"Sometimes the boys come up and we all smoke."

Seth said, "No offense, Evan, but if you happen to dig smoking—"

I just started laughing. I'm not sure why. Arlette, Seth, Randy, Emile, Claude, Jean, Jacques, the Chief, the helicopter pilot, the woman with the lost kids, the Cuban dungeon, my landlord, my air-conditioner, Sonya, Minna, the heat, the humidity, I don't know.

"Oh, what the hell," I said, gasping. "Why not?"

I hadn't smoked anything in ages. I had smoked cigarettes for about three years before I was wounded in Korea. Shortly thereafter I discovered that when you were awake around the clock, you smoked around the clock, and with my body deprived of eight hours' abstinence from tobacco, I rapidly developed a chronic cough and sore throat. When cutting down didn't work, I quit cold. That turned out to be infinitely easier than I had suspected, and I discovered that not smoking was better than smoking, and that was that.

Then about seven or eight years ago a girl turned me on to marijuana, and I smoked now and then for a period of about a year and a half. Toward the end I found that I was no longer getting the pleasant giggling highs that I'd had in the beginning, but that I was more and more frequently ending up with deep, moody, brooding highs, long sieges of introspection and philosophical self-analysis that were as often as not rather depressing. I decided that I didn't have to smoke to get depressed, and that was the end of that experiment.

Since that time the closest I ever came to any kind of habit was on a trek through Thailand and Laos, in the course of which I found myself becoming mildly addicted to betel nut. If betel nut were available in the States, I might have stayed hooked, but it isn't.

I am not entirely certain why I decided to smoke marijuana that night in Montreal. If the Chief were the sort of bore who demanded written reports of his agents' activities, that would have to be one of the many items I would neglect to mention. The determining factors, I suppose, were the great load of frustration I had built up cruising back from the Cuban Pavilion and the air of lunacy that overhung Arlette's apartment. Add to that my usual list-making pattern—write everything down, read it over, get drunk—and the idea of turning on made its own sort of sense.

I might add, too, that I hoped I would hit on a deep, thoughtful high, and that my mind, liberated from its usual patterns of thought, might chance upon something that would put everything right, some mental philosopher's stone to translate all the madness of the world into something meaningful. I might add that, but it wouldn't be true. There were only a few hours left before Betty Battenberg turned into hamburger, and Minna had probably already been sold into white slavery in Afghanistan, and the Union Corse would get me if the Royal Canadian Mounted Police didn't, and to tell you the truth, I just didn't care any more about anything.

This happens. Tighten a muscle long enough, and eventually it will relax of its own accord and remain utterly flaccid. Emotional muscles adhere to the same law. I had worried too much about too many things for a little too long, and the worry muscle had simply ceased to function. I no longer gave a damn. If pot would turn the next two or three hours into a restful groove, I was all for it.

Seth rolled the stuff. He kept the grass and a packet of Zig-Zag cigarette papers in a plastic bag in his pocket, the same sort of plastic bag housewives use for leftovers and teenagers for condoms. He used two papers for each cigarette so the resulting product would smoke slowly, and he rolled them thin and tight. During my own viper period I never learned to do this, and used to buy packs of cigarettes and shake the tobacco out of the paper tubes, replacing it with the grass. I watched Seth roll the pot, and Arlette found some music on the radio that, if not psychedelic, was at least bearable, and we turned off most of the lights and lit up, smoking the joints one at a time, passing them from hand to hand, going through all the happy ritual of the pot mystique. The years, I noted, had added a few variations; the boys had a way of cupping both hands over the cigarette end and inhaling simultaneously through nose and mouth that I had never come across before. I suppose that was to prevent any smoke from getting wasted.

I had enough trouble smoking as I had in the past. The grass burned hot despite its double wrapper. Randy said he thought someone must have cut it slightly with green tea, which doesn't change the taste but scorches your throat. The back of my throat was raw by the third drag, and a pulse went on beating there for a long time.

There was no sudden moment when I went from straight to high, but a variety of sensations that began very gradually and increased steadily. I became intensely aware of things—I followed several different musical instruments simultaneously on the radio, I concentrated on various portions of my own body and became keenly interested in such bits of excitement as the play of warm air on my hands, the expansion and contraction of my rib cage as I breathed, the relentless movement of gases in my intestinal tract.

The boys were talking, but I couldn't pay any attention to them. I could listen to every word, very much wrapped up in what they were saying, but my mind would wander off and I would forget their words almost as quickly as I heard them. I had no urge to reply, or to talk about anything at all, or to listen to what anyone else had to say. They seemed to be having one of those long, involved pot conversations with baklavalike layers of meaning and unmeaning, and I'm sure they enjoyed it very much, but it was not my kind of high. My mind was telling me it had things it wanted to think about, and if I tried to fight it, I would only get confused. I didn't fight. I stretched out on the floor in the relaxation posture and let myself get loose.

I had trouble at first. My head was on bare flooring, and my pot-heightened sensibility made this contact very uncomfortable. After a while (perhaps a minute, perhaps an hour; my time sense had disappeared completely) I sat up, took off my shirt, and used it as a thin pillow. Then I relaxed in the usual yoga fashion, and the pot and the Yoga reinforced one another, and I went in very deep, very deep.

I cannot tell you precisely what happened after that, because the experience does not lend itself to verbal description. I didn't actually *think* about anything. You couldn't call it thought. I was, in a sense, a screen on which a movie was being shown. There was an endless parade of images, connections made and connections broken, spirited mental leaps, occasional false starts, a touch perhaps of madness, and, well, something else that defies explanation.

Once I saw a Haight-Ashbury hippie interviewed on television. He had taken LSD and wound up in a mental hospital. He explained that the acid trip had been worthwhile, that it taught him some extraordinary things about himself. What, asked the interviewer, had it taught him? "I know now," said the acidhead, "that the present is where the past and the future meet."

At the time, I couldn't avoid the suspicion that someone might have come to this pinnacle of wisdom without dropping acid. Now I'm not so certain. I'm willing to concede perception to that hippie. The fact that he was unable to articulate the insights he hit on does not necessarily mean that they weren't there. He simply didn't know the words that went with that particular tune.

I do know that when my high lost the first portion of its edge, I turned from mental to physical gymnastics and tried some yogic techniques that I had never previously mastered. I made my left eye look to the left while my right eye was looking off to the right, and I contracted various abdominal muscles groups that I had never before had voluntary control over, and at one point I either stopped my heartbeat or thought I did, which may or may not amount to the same thing, depending upon your point of view. I guess I could have lived just as well without being able to perform these little tricks, and I can't honestly say how they might be of value in time to come, but they pleased me no end; I thought of them as physical proof of the validity of the mental exercises I had undergone. If I could really manage exercises while high that I could not perform otherwise, then perhaps it followed that the mental connections I had made might have a certain amount of substance, that they might be more than a waking dream.

Well. That, in any case, is about how it went. When I came out of the trance—you'd have to call it that—I was out of it all the way, wide awake, refreshed, alert. The radio was still going, bringing in nothing but static now. I hadn't noticed the static before. I turned off the radio and checked the clock. It was a quarter to seven. The high had lasted a little under three hours.

On the bed Seth and Randy and Arlette slept nude in delicate obscenity. They had evidently spent their high making some sort of triangular love, as unaware of my presence as I was of theirs. I drew the tigerskin over them and went into the bathroom and showered and shaved.

I got dressed again and put up water for a fresh pot of coffee. The three of them went right on sleeping with occasional groping noises issuing from beneath the sheet. I ignored these insofar as possible. I measured out coffee and poured the water through it and hunted around for something to eat. I was suddenly ravenous and the cupboard was bare. I settled ultimately for a bread sandwich, a slice of whole wheat between two slices of white. It wasn't very much better than it sounds.

At eight o'clock I carried three cups of coffee to the bed, set them down upon the bedside table, and shook each of the bed's occupants in turn until they were sufficiently awake to accept coffee. Seth and Randy woke easily, and Arlette was not nearly so foggy as she had been in the past.

She looked at me and blushed. The boys didn't notice, I don't think; it probably would not have occurred to them to be embarrassed about their little homage to troilism. I'm sure they didn't regard it as an orgy or anything of the sort. Just three good friends getting high together and being friendly and warm and tender to one another. For my part, it was just another item on the lengthening list of things I did not really give a damn about. But Arlette, the Oft-Made of Orleans, was the sort of angel who manages to behave like a free spirit without ever quite feeling like one. I didn't know how to respond to her, unable to make up my mind whether it would be more insulting to scorn her as a slut or convey to her the idea that I didn't really care.

So instead I said, "I woke you early for a reason. We have twelve hours before the Queen hits the fan."

Seth looked at me. "You straight, Evan?"

"Straight as a hoop snake. We have twelve hours. That's plenty of time. I got it all figured out. We'll fix things so they pop the right way, and then we'll pick up on Minna before the sparks go out."

Seth and Randy exchanged glances. Seth said, "I think he's still stoned out of his gourd."

"Sounds like."

But they were both wrong. I knew exactly what I meant, and I had a hunch it would work.

14

Arlette didn't have a map of the Montreal area on hand. She offered to go buy one, but I chose to save time by sketching a rough map on a sheet of notebook paper. The four of us sat around the kitchen table while I outlined the route the royal barge would take.

At a bend in the river, I made an X. "This is where the ambush is scheduled to take place," I said. "Up here on the right there's a sort of hill that provides a perfect vantage point. And down here"—I made a pencil mark—"is a natural inlet, a pocket bay just large enough to hold a motorboat."

Randy said, "Question."

"Go ahead."

"Which check mark is the Texas Book Depository?"

I looked at him, and he apologized. I pointed again with the pencil. "Now this is how they're going to do it," I said. "One man—Claude—will be on top of the hill with a pair of binoculars and a rifle. He'll pick up the barge just as it approaches Point X and fire a volley of three shots across the bow. That serves two purposes—it identifies the barge positively for the other three and should also slow it down some, if not stop it entirely.

"As soon as Claude starts shooting; the rest of them go into their act. Jean and Jacques Berton will be here in the clump of brush. Or next to it, or in back of it, whatever. They have a machine gun—"

"Sweet Jesus."

"Exactly. They'll begin firing as soon as Claude goes into action. The way things are set up, they'll be able to triangulate on the barge. With shots coming from two different directions, the captain won't be able to get out of the line of fire. He's almost certain to freeze."

"Got it," Seth said. "The hill is the Texas Book Depository, and the clump of brush is the Grassy Knoll."

"Whatever way you want. There's more coming. Once the shooting starts up, Emile begins sailing from the cove—"

"Sailing?"

"He'll be in the sheltered cove in a motorboat, a fast one. He'll have a pistol, but that's the least of it. The boat will be overflowing with explosives. Plastique, dynamite, God knows what else. While the triangulated gunfire freezes the barge, Emile will set out for it at top speed on a collision course." I sighed and shook my head. "He's arranging things so that the explosive charge goes off on impact."

Arlette was hearing the details for the first time and seemed staggered by them. She kept murmuring little oaths in French. The boys' reaction was ambivalent; they seemed torn between horror at the enormity of the deed and admiration for the sweet simplicity of it.

Randy said, "Good-bye, Queenie."

"That's the general idea."

"I don't see how they can miss, man. Unless there's a mess of police boats for escorts—"

"There probably will be. It doesn't matter—with all the confusion that the gunshots will generate, it's highly unlikely that anybody will even notice Emile's boat, much less do anything to stop it. He'll have the throttle tied all the way down once he gets going, so that even if he's shot dead, the boat will go along on its merry way."

"I'd love to meet the clown who planned this."

I coughed. "Well," I said, "I planned some of it—"

"You?"

I nodded, equally proud and ashamed. When we'd had our planning session Saturday afternoon, I had added a few refinements, on the theory that if one was going to do something, one might as well do it right. I was a little sorry about that now. The plan was almost too right.

I raised the pencil again. "Now here's what we do," I said, with what was supposed to be contagious confidence in my voice. "Timing is very important. The Queen is scheduled to arrive at the fairgrounds at eight thirty. If she follows that schedule, and it's logical to assume that she will, then the barge will reach Point X somewhere between seven fifty and eight ten. The assassins will be at their posts from seven o'clock on, and they'll expect to hit the barge at eight, give or take a few minutes. If the barge isn't there on time, then we have a chance."

Arlette looked at me. "But they will simply wait—"

"I've got that figured out. Let's take one thing at a time. The first step is to delay the royal barge. The longer it's delayed, the better our chances look." I pointed the pencil at the boys. "That's where you two come in."

"Us?"

"Right."

"How?"

"You delay the barge right here," I said, indicating a spot a few inches to the west on my little map. "There's a narrows here—the river dips around an island to the south, which I didn't put on the map, but it's right around there somewhere. That's where you stop the good lady."

"With what?"

"A demonstration. *Queen Elizabeth—Stop The Shitty War In Vietnam.* Something like that. It doesn't—"

Seth was looking at me oddly. "Evan," he said, "just what in hell can Queen Elizabeth do about the war in Vietnam?"

"Nothing. The point is—"

"I mean, England isn't even *in* the war, for Christ's sake."

"I know. The point is—"

"I mean, of all the people to picket, I don't see—"

"Will you please let me tell you what the point is?"

"I'm sorry."

"God in Heaven," I said. I drew a breath. "I don't really care whether the demonstration is about the Vietnam war or the British presence in Aden or Hong Kong or whatever the hell you want. I said Vietnam because I figured you already had plenty of signs made. We don't have much time."

"I'm sorry, Evan."

"And if you interrupt every ten seconds, we'll have even less time."

"I said I was sorry."

"Mmmm," I said. Evan Michael Tanner, Leader of Men. "You organize a demonstration," I went on, more calmly this time. "Get everybody you possibly can in on it, the more the merrier. Mass at the narrows at seven thirty. No earlier, or the police might break you up and send you home before the Queen arrives. You won't have trouble spotting the royal barge. It will be flying English and Canadian flags and will probably have an escort. Once the barge comes into view, do your bit." I thought for a moment. "On second thought, hold off until the barge enters the narrows. Then do your bit in front of it. Otherwise someone might decide to get clever and take an end run around the island."

"Got it. What do we do, just make a lot of noise and wave the signs?"

"No. They'd sail right by."

"That's what I thought."

"You'll need boats. You'll have to form a regular boat bridge across the channel. They'll break you up sooner or later, but that should give us all the time we need."

"To do what?"

"There's no time now. Get rowboats, canoes, rafts, anything that can float. And as large a crowd as you can put together. And—"

"We'll get busted," Randy said.

"Probably, but the charges won't even amount to anything. You might get fined, you might even have to do ten days. I'll take care of the fines—"

He was shaking his head. "You don't get it. We don't mind the fines, or even doing a short bit. That's not the point. The thing is, what they would probably do, in fact what they already did to a cat who got picked up for the possession of pot, is ship us back to the States as undesirable aliens. We don't have Canadian citizenship or anything. So getting busted might mean getting sent home."

"Which would mean the draft board," Seth said.

"Which would mean Leavenworth," Randy said.

"For five years."

"Or Vietnam."

"For as long as it takes to get killed."

"Oh," I said. I thought about it. "This pacifist organization you belong to—does it have any Canadian members?"

"Quite a few."

"And there are probably some other political groups, local ones, that you have ties with?"

"Oh, sure. There's the Labor Youth League, and there's—"

"Just so there are some, that's all I'm interested in. Suppose you just set up the demonstration without participating in it? Suppose you stocked it with local people? You could stay on the sidelines and do the planning and set up the timing, and then you could slip away as soon as things got started."

"It might work."

"I like that better," I went on. "Because I could probably use you later on. You think you could round up a sufficient number of Canadians to stop that boat? It would take at least thirty, and fifty would be better. There's not much time."

"We can do it."

"Are you sure?"

"No sweat. There's not that much really active political work going on, and plenty of our crowd would be glad to join in. Especially when they realize they'll be saving the Queen's life."

"Uh-uh."

"What?"

"You can't tell anyone that," I said. "Not a word. That's the whole point—if we just wanted to keep the woman alive, we could tip off the police and let justice be done. The assassination would be stopped and that would be the end of it. The important thing is to louse it up without lousing it up, if you follow me. Nobody can know a thing."

"They wouldn't talk."

"They'd talk the minute they were arrested."

He scratched his head. "You could be right. That makes it harder, though. Fifty Canadians who have to protest without knowing why. I think we can forget the Vietnam angle, Evan. They'd never go for it. Maybe Aden would do it, unless they happen to support the British stand in Aden—"

"Some of them probably do," I agreed. "Make it Modonoland."

"I never heard of it."

"It's one of the new African nations. Protest the British policy on Modonoland. The signs could say something like *Hands off Modonoland*, that sort of thing."

"Sounds good," Seth said. "Uh, just so we know, I mean, like, if anybody asks—"

"What?"

"Well, man, I hate to seem uninformed, but just what *is* the British policy on Modonoland?"

"I don't think they have one."

"Huh?"

"There hasn't been any trouble in Modonoland," I said. "Not that I know of. If Britain has had any involvement with the country, I never heard about it. So who'll disagree with you? Oh, I suppose one or two contrary types will insist that Britain has every right to be in Modonoland, but everyone else will go along with you. They can't support a policy that doesn't exist, but they can certainly attack it."

"That's brilliant."

"Think you can handle it?"

"I hope so. It's what—nine-thirty now? And you want us to be in position by seven thirty? That's nine hours—"

"Ten hours."

"Well, whatever it is. Ten hours. Five people an hour, that shouldn't be too much of a hassle."

"And boats. Don't forget the boats. And it would probably be a good idea if the two of you went on ahead to the narrows to look the place over in advance. Determine just how many boats you'll need and how you want to stage it. Make sure your demonstrators know where the place is and have them all meet there. Have them come individually or in small groups. Otherwise one inquisitive cop could spoil the whole show in advance."

"We always work demonstrations that way."

"Good."

They got to their feet. Then Seth turned to me. "How much of an edge do you want, Evan? How long do you expect us to hold them?"

"As long as possible, naturally." I shrugged. "That's really as much as I can say. A half hour would be good. Fifteen minutes might be enough, but that would be cutting it a little close. The longer the barge is delayed, the better our chances are of cooling things at Point X."

"How are you going to handle that, by the way?"

"I'm going to try to get them to blow up the wrong boat. The idea is—" I broke off. "To hell with it, there's no time now. If it works, you'll know what happened. If it doesn't, it won't matter what was supposed to happen. Do what you can to set things up. Remember, the more demonstrators the better, and the longer you can hold the barge the better. When something goes wrong—"

"You mean *if* something goes wrong."

"If and when, try to let me know about it. Either Arlette or I will be here for most of the afternoon. If anything goes wrong at the last minute, I don't know what to tell you to do."

"Tip the fuzz."

"No, don't do that no matter what happens. Well, let me amend that. If you learn that I'm killed between now and then—"

"Are you serious?"

"Anything's possible. I could get hit by a bus or shot resisting arrest or I don't know what. If you hear that, you might as well blab to the police. But make sure they listen to you if you do. Police are apt to take down a statement and type up three copies and file them, and let the Queen get killed in the meantime. If you have to sing, sing out loud and clear."

They both nodded soberly. And Seth said, "This is for real, isn't it."

"Right. No games."

"We'll make it work, Evan. That barge is going to stay put for half an hour if I have to use myself for the anchor."

I looked at him and Randy. They were pretty good at kidding, but they weren't kidding now. The flip-hip easiness was on the shelf. They knew what they had to do and they were going to do it. They also knew what would happen to them if a wheel came off, and they wouldn't be able to forget it over the next ten hours, but I had a hunch they would carry through regardless.

And I smiled then at the thought that the States was overflowing with cretins who had already written these kids off as gutless wonders, scared of getting their asses shot off in Southeast Asia. And I thought back to my own time in Korea, and thought of some of the men in my outfit, and of myself.

At that age hardly anyone really worries about death. I certainly hadn't. I had known that the possibility of dying existed, and when I was in actual front-line combat and watched men catch bullets on either side of me, I was certainly scared, but I don't think I ever honestly conceived the idea of my own personal death. It was something that happened to other people; I was eighteen years old and I was going to live forever, or to be fifty, anyway, which at that age amounts to the same thing.

I certainly didn't think about dying when I went in to the service. Or during training. One doesn't. At that age a jail sentence or forced exile or ostracism are all scarier than the statistical possibility of death in combat.

Gutless wonders? No, the cowards played a different game. They worked a psychiatrist for a certification that would get them a 4-F, or they found a way to flunk the physical, or they got married and hatched a little draft deferment. Or they thought about Leavenworth and Canada and how their families would take it and what kind of job opportunities would exist for draft-dodgers, and then they shrugged like good German soldiers and let themselves be drafted.

"Evan? You said something about us getting together afterward."

"Oh." I took a sip of coffee. "Right. We'll need you again later on when we rescue Minna, but—"

"Not tonight?"

"Definitely. The only way to get out of this mess is to do everything at once. I'll want your help, but I don't know where or when."

"That's a song."

"I know. Look, call me right here at six o'clock, whether things are going well or not. By that time I'll have the planning down pat and I'll tell you where to meet me. And"— I hauled out my wallet, passed them a few bills—"take this. Don't walk when you can take cabs. Time is more important than money right now."

"We have some bread."

"Take it anyway. You might have to rent boats. Don't cut corners, don't try to save money. Just stop that barge."

"Right."

They left. Gutless wonders, I thought. Hippies. Cultural

dropouts. Draft-dodgers. Pot-smokers.

Sure.

"They're going to be good," I told Arlette.

"They are good boys, cherished one." And then I guess she must have considered some of the ways in which they were good, because she blushed. "Evan," she said, "I disgust you, is it not so? Ah, what you must think of me! But my cherished Evan . . ."

If she was going to be any good at all in the next ten hours, we had to get this out of the way once and for all. I said, "It was fun, wasn't it?"

"Pardon?"

"In bed, while everyone was high. It was nice and warm and gentle and friendly, right? It was fun. It felt good."

"I am the name of a pig."

"Just answer the question."

"But of course it felt good. It was . . . I cannot talk about it."

"Then don't."

"You do not hate me?"

"Of course not."

"You do not find me despicable?"

"I find you delightful. You are being silly. Is a woman to be despised because she has had a lover, because she is not a virgin?"

"No, but—"

"Is she to be despised because in the course of her life she has had more than one lover?"

"No, but—"

"She could have ten, twenty, thirty lovers, is it not so?"

"Yes, but—"

"So if she should happen to be with two of those lovers at the same time, is this reason for despising her? A mere temporal coincidence? Certainly not!"

"Once even there were three," she said dreamily. "Oh, Evan! Then you do not detest me? You still love me?"

"I still love you," I said. I took a very deep breath. "Now let's forget all that, shall we? We've got a lot to do, you and I."

15

I tried to go over the whole operation with Arlette. This didn't work out very well. She didn't have the right kind of mind for it, and kept interrupting with idiot questions about things I had already explained to her. Other times she tried to rush ahead and asked about points that I was saving for later on. When I blew up, she insisted that I did not love her and that I despised her for making love with Seth and Randy. It was hard going for a while, until I realized that Arlette was not the type to cope with a long-range plan. She had to deal with one specific task at a time, and it only complicated matters to explain to her why she was supposed to do thus and so. You don't tell a horse why you want to turn right, you just pull the reins in that direction (or in the other direction; I still don't remember which is right).

It was thus with Arlette. If she had to think about something, she was very likely to foul it up. Once I'd figured this out, things went a whole lot smoother.

"I need a pistol," I said.

"Must we shoot someone?"

"Forget it. I need a pistol. Do you have one?"

"No. Emile—"

"I don't think we should ask Emile for a pistol."

"But perhaps—"

She was making a beeline for another tangent. I held up my hand. "Stop. We need a pistol. Not from Emile. Can you purchase one?"

"No. One must—"

"Forget it. Can you obtain one from someone who is not in the MNQ?"

"No."

"Can you get one from some member besides the four who are in on the assassination? Someone who has some guns tucked away for an eventual rising?"

"Henri has a great stock of weapons. Did you meet him? He was—"

"Then, he won't miss one pistol. That's good. Get one from him, preferably forty-five or thirty-eight caliber, preferably an automatic, but take what you can get. Just one gun should do."

"He will ask why I want it."

"Tell him you were ordered to get it. If he asks more questions, tell him that is all you are allowed to tell him. The simplest lies are best. Henri doesn't know about the assassination? Forget the question, it doesn't matter. Just get the gun."

"Yes."

"And make sure it's loaded," I called after her.

As I said, she was fine once you knew how to handle her. She was back in twenty minutes with a fully loaded Marley automatic plus an extra seven-shot clip for insurance. It was a .32, which was lighter than I would have liked but still heavy enough to do most jobs. The gun was made in Japan, like everything else. I wondered if I would be able to hit anything with it and hoped I would never have to try.

I hefted the gun in my hand. "Perfect," I said. "I made a few phone calls while you were out. What I want you to do now is go down to the Link-Wright Shipping Company. Look lost and helpless and beautiful. You have to find out what the barge will look like and when it's going to reach Point X."

"The royal barge?"

"God, no. We already know that. The other one, the target." I thought for a moment. "Okay, here's a thought. Your kid brother has some horrible disease. Something crippling. Make it muscular dystrophy. Anyone who can't sympathize with a dystrophic kid is beyond redemption. He can't get to the fair because he's crippled. Do you understand?"

"I think so."

"So he wants to see the boat. You can see the river from your house, and he'll be watching tonight, and he wants to know when the boat will pass by and what it will look like, so he'll know when he sees it. Got that?"

"I think so. I shall tell him we live at Point X—"

"Don't do that. Forget Point X, please." I stabbed a finger at the map. "Tell him you live about here, figure out something that fits. You know the city better than I do. But find out those two things, what the boat will look like and when to expect it. If we know when it will get here, we can figure out the rest of the timing pretty well."

"All right. My crippled brother has musical atrophy and

cannot go to Expo, and he wishes to see the boat, and . . ."

We went through the story until she had it as well as she ever would, and then I wrote out the address of Link-Wright Shipping and sent her on her way. The story hadn't struck me as particularly brilliant when I thought of it, and the more I heard it, the less I liked it, but I felt she could probably pull it off. I made her fix her makeup and splash on a little perfume before she left. With all of that sex going for her, I didn't think she would have much trouble. They would probably give her an 8-by-10 glossy of the boat and an invitation to dine at the captain's table.

While she was off charming them at Link-Wright I worked on her phony ID. I still had that silly Expo passport, and one of the pages for visa stamps was still blank. It was just the right paper, with all of those swirly lines in it that suggest all the trappings of bureaucracy. I removed the page and cut out a neat rectangle about 2½" by 4" and popped it into Arlette's portable typewriter. Then I checked the page I'd practiced on earlier. It's not easy to make a typewriter produce something that looks as though it were printed. A varitype machine will do a good job, and an electric is fair, but all she had was a rickety portable. At least I had fixed things so that the lines more or less came out the same length. I certainly wasn't going to create something equal to my beautiful forged passport (which I could probably forget forever now, its having been left behind in our hotel room); but if things went well, the ID would get little more than a quick glance in a dark room, and it might stand up under those conditions.

What I typed was:

DOMINION OF CANADA
Department of Public Security

This is to identify the bearer
_____ as an agent in
good standing of the Foreign National Section, Department of
Public Security, accredited via
the Dominion Secrets Acts
(1954) and fully empowered
thereunder.

photo   rt. thumb

_____
J.B. Westley
Int. Director

I shifted the slip so that it was slightly off-center and, using a lighter touch, typed in *Suzanne Lafitte* on the proper line. I used a ball-point pen to sign J.B. Westley's name on yet another line. I studied the result and decided that it lacked something. Maybe a little sketch of a maple leaf in one corner . . .

I practiced drawing maple leaves on some scrap paper, and they all came out looking more like palm trees. So I let that go until Arlette came back with a description of the boat, an estimate of its time of arrival at her mythical residence, and a seemingly endless story about the truly charming men she had met at Link-Wright Shipping.

I figured out the probable time differential between her fabled home and Point X and came up with a half-educated guess that it would reach the target area around twenty to eight. I couldn't decide whether that was good or bad. It meant that it would be in position quite a few minutes before Emile and his friends expected to get the game started, which was bad, but it also meant that we had a little margin for error, and that Seth and Randy wouldn't have to delay the Queen quite so long. I decided that the good out-weighed the bad, and then I decided that we were going to play it the same way no matter what, so the hell with it. I showed her my little paper creation and she stared at it, read it, turned it over, studied its back, turned it over again, peered closely at the Westley signature, and asked me what it was.

"Your identification."

"I do not understand. Who is this Westley? And this Suzanne, this Mademoiselle Lafitte, who is she?"

"She's you," I said. "Don't worry about it, I'll explain it later. I want you to practice writing Suzanne Lafitte. Go ahead."

She wrote it a few times and I looked it over. I just wanted to make sure she could do it without misspelling it. Then I had her sign the card. I had pressed down harder with the pen when I wrote Westley's name, so it looked as though two different pens had been used.

"Perfect," I said. "Now I'll need a very tiny photo of you. Do you have one?"

She found some snapshots, but they all had scenery in the background. I sent her on her way again, telling her to get her picture taken at one of the 4-Poses-For-25¢ booths at the Dorchester Boulevard bus terminal. She brought back four ghastly poses that looked enough unlike her to be official, along with the things I had told her to buy—a stamp pad, a rubber stamp that would print any number from 0000001 to 9999999, a tube of rubber cement, a packet of razor blades, and a large red leatherette photo album.

"Perfect," I said. "Perfect."

She didn't say a word, bless her heart. She watched in silence as I trimmed one of the photos to the size of the space on the card and glued it carefully in place. I set the rubber stamp at 8839970 and stamped the card twice, once below the Suzanne Lafitte signature and once along the left-hand edge. (The number was one I selected apparently at random, but I happen to remember it now because I later realized that it was the number of "Hector's Lounge," which started all of this mess. Make of this what you will.)

The stamp pad also served to get Arlette's fingerprint impressed in the proper square. Her right thumbprint, to be precise. We tried it four times on scrap paper before I got the hang of it. It seemed to work best if I held her thumb and pressed it to the paper myself, and that was how we finally did it.

Then I looted the photo album. I removed the insides and cut the cover open. The leatherette was wrapped around a sheet of very thick cardboard. I cut out a pair of 5 by 7 cardboard rectangles, then cut out a large piece of leatherette and glued the cardboard chunks to it, one above the other. Then I glued the card in place on the lower section of cardboard.

It looked phony as hell to me. The typing was the main problem—it gave the whole thing a homemade look. My Croat Nationalist friend in New York would have been disgusted with it. The Armenian genius in Athens would have thrown up either his hands or his dinner at the sight of it. I almost said this aloud, then decided against it. Arlette was going to have to use the damned thing, and it was pointless to destroy her confidence in it.

I moistened my hands and smudged it a little in strategic spots. Then I cut out a piece of acetate from the leaves of the photo album and cemented it into place over the card. At least I tried to; the rubber cement wouldn't bond to the plastic. I had to send Arlette out for some plastic cement before I could get it to work.

By the time I had trimmed the leatherette and performed the final gluing operations, it really didn't look so bad after all. The final product was a purse-sized red leather case that opened up to reveal an ID card complete with photo and thumbprint and signature. It *did* look like credentials of some sort, and there was no fear that some clown would compare it with the genuine article. Because as far as I knew, there was no Department of Public Security, no Foreign National Section, no Dominion Secrets Act (1954), no J.B. Westley, Int. Director, and no Suzanne Lafitte.

"I think it'll do," I said. "How does it look to you?"

"Formidable. I do not understand."

"You'll understand when the time comes."

"But how is this to prevent the assassination? I cannot show this to Claude or Jean or Jacques or Emile. They have known me for too long, Evan. They would never believe that I am this Mademoiselle Lafitte. They know that I am Arlette Sazerac, they know that I am a faithful allegiant of the Movement Nation de Québec." She frowned suddenly. "I *was* a faithful allegiant. Now suddenly I am a traitor."

"You are a true patriot. You are doing what is best for the

movement."

"It is so. It must be so." She touched my arm. "But you have not explained! How is this, this false identification, this Lafitte, how is it to prevent the assassination?"

"That's not what it's for. It's to rescue Minna from the Cubans."

"I do not understand." She furrowed her brow, trying desperately to think. "How is it possible to do everything at once?"

I thought of my Mickey Mouse list. Minna, assassination, heroin, cops. I had a variation on the time-tested formula. You listed all your chores in order, and then you killed some time and smoked some pot, and then you took a deep breath and a giant step and did everything at once.

"How?" she still wanted to know.

"I'll tell you later," I lied. I looked at the clock; it was past noon already. "There's no time now, cherished one. There are things that must be done at once. There is a man at the fairgrounds, you will have to seek him out and make contact with him. And I will need some preparations to disguise myself, some cosmetics, a variety of articles. I will be going outside while it is still light out, and it would not be good if I were arrested—"

"It would be a disaster!"

"I agree. Put the ID down, that's a good girl. Now let me see what you ought to do first . . ."

What she did first was make the rounds of the neighborhood tobacconists, buying three or four plastic roll-up tobacco pouches at each shop. (This was not done for the sake of subtlety; I didn't really care what some tobacconist might think if she bought twenty pouches from him. She bought only three or four in each shop because nobody had more than that on hand.) She came right back with them, and while she was off on another errand I parceled out the three cans of heroin into the twenty pouches. When I was all done, I had about a tablespoonful left over, and I spent longer than I care to admit brooding about it before realizing that the world could live without it. I flushed it down the toilet. *Junkies are crawling up walls in Harlem,* said a voice deep within my brain, *and you flush heroin down the toilet. Children are starving in India and you didn't finish your Brussels sprouts. Families are starving in Brussels and you didn't finish your Indian summer. Old people are starving in Sumatra and you didn't finish your winter wheat. Arlette is starving for affection and you didn't make love to her in the winter of our discontent made glorious summer by this son of Yorktown ladies sing this song, doo dah, doo dah—*

I raced into the bathroom and stood under the shower. Doo dah, doo dah. I let the cold water pound down on my head until the little voice in there stopped yammering. I wondered how much the heroin I had flushed away was worth, and I wondered why I was wondering about something that irrelevant, and I decided I hadn't spent enough time under the shower. I soaked my head a little longer and let everything calm down. *Just a spoonful of powder makes the Madison go round, the moccasin go brown, the Mattachine go down, just a spoonful—* More cold water and a brisk rub with a towel.

My disguise was a major problem. Ideally I needed one that I could switch on and off at will, so that I could avoid being recognized while I was out in the open without looking like a stranger when I joined the assassination party at Point X. I kept getting ideas toward this end, and they kept not working. I would send Arlette out for something new—now a wig, now a monster Halloween mask, now this and now that—but the conveniently removable disguises all had one thing in common. They looked like disguises, and policemen are apt to take an interest in people who look disguised.

The time wasn't completely wasted. Arlette's wild-goose chases at least kept her out of my hair while I taped up the pouches of heroin and sewed them into my clothing. The jacket got the greater portion of them. I took up the lining, flattened the pouches and sewed them here and there inside it, then replaced the lining. The end product of all this effort was nothing geared to win hysterical applause from a tailor's convention—I wound up with a pretty lumpy jacket. Still, it was a way to transport the junk with some degree of secrecy, and it left my hands free.

It took the Frankenstein mask to convince me that a removable disguise was an unrealistic goal. I put it on and Arlette went into a laughing fit. I couldn't see the expression on her face—I couldn't see anything because my eyes didn't happen to be placed as close together as Frankenstein's—but the laughter came through the mask. The air didn't; I was sweating furiously in less than ten seconds. I took off the mask and told Arlette I didn't think it would do.

"But it is lovely," she insisted. "You must someday wear such a mask when we make love."

I sent her out again—it was that or hit her—and she came

back with a long list of things and helped me use them to remake my face. We started off with my hair, cutting off quite a bit of it, raising the sideburns three-eighths of an inch, and working black dye into what hair remained. I thought I looked pretty terrible, but Arlette insisted that it wasn't that bad.

"I myself could become a blonde," she said.

"No."

"But otherwise they will recognize me."

"Arlette, they're not *looking* for you. That's the whole point."

"But they will not recognize you at Point X, and they will recognize me."

"They're supposed to."

"They will see us together and wonder who I am with. They will—"

I shifted gears. "Arlette, the picture on your identification card is a girl with dark hair. It wouldn't do to—"

"I could wear a wig, then—"

"Arlette—"

"—or we could have a new photograph taken. Evan, is something wrong? You feel I would appear unattractive as a blonde? You do not think I would have more fun?"

Fool, I told myself, you've been trying to *reason* with her! I said, "We shall someday find out, my apple of love. We will taste the fruits of love together, you with blonde hair and I in my Frankenstein mask." I swallowed. "But you must help me now. I am not finished with my disguise, and you must help me."

I didn't need her help. I just needed her to shut the hell up. I sat in front of her mirror and played with all the nice toys she had brought me. I used theatrical putty on my nose and ears. I had once read somewhere that ears are the most difficult feature to disguise, and that trained law-enforcement officers always pay close attention to people's ears. They're way ahead of me on that score. I hardly ever notice ears unless they stick out or one of them is missing, or something like that.

So I puttied my ears. I didn't want to do anything extreme. I figured that funny-looking ears would attract attention almost as well as the Frankenstein mask, but on second thought I decided that all ears are funny-looking to a greater or lesser degree. I enlarged the lobes of mine, and built things up here and there, and gave the tops a slight peak. The hard part was making them both come out the same, which, now that I think about it, was probably unnecessary, as few people see both of one's ears at the same time. I did a good job, though, and when I was through, Arlette told me I looked different. I didn't see it myself. "You mean my ears look different," I said.

"So it must be, but I do not recall how they looked before. No, your *face* has changed."

I guess the police know what they're doing, at least insofar as ears are concerned.

I fixed my nose, too, making it a little longer and straightening out the slight bump just below the bridge. I preferred my ears as they had been before, but I had to admit that the new nose was more becoming than the original model.

"Your eyebrows, Evan."

I had forgotten to dye them. I did this, getting only a little bit of hair dye in my eye and swearing only for a few minutes. I tried on the clear glass spectacles Arlette had bought me. The only trouble with them was that they looked fake. The light reflected oddly off the flat surface of the glass. The sunglasses were much better and hid my eyes in the bargain but might look odd after dark, assuming I still wanted to be disguised by then.

I put my new cap on my head. It was similar to the wino's cap but infinitely cleaner. Too clean, I decided. It looked as if it had been hatched that morning. I threw it on the floor and stepped on it while Arlette looked at me as though I had gone suddenly mad.

The phone rang. I grabbed it, and it was Seth. "Oh, no," I said. "It can't be six yet. It's impossible."

"It isn't. You okay, man?"

It was three thirty and once I found that out, I was okay and said so. I asked him if anything had gone wrong.

"Nothing serious. We've got twenty-three bodies for sure and a batch of maybes. From past experience, I'd say one out of three maybes will show. That's in the States, in a typical antiwar march. It could be different with Canadians for a Modonoland protest, but I don't know whether it would be more or less."

"You'll know in a couple of hours."

"I'm hip. The reason I called—"

"How are you doing on boats?"

"Not too bad. Randy's out on a lead now, and there's a chick from Nova Scotia who's getting in touch with a friend who's supposed to know somebody. You know how it goes. I don't honestly know how many we have lined up, but I think we'll make it. I'll know better at six o'clock."

"Good."

"Uh, the reason I called—"

"How about money? Are you running low?"

"No, that's no problem. Evan, why I called—"

"I'm sorry." I was turning into Arlette. "Go ahead."

"Well, this is ridiculous, but how the hell do you spell Modonoland? We're lettering some signs now and nobody knows how it's spelled, hardly anybody ever heard of it. It's not in any reference books around here. Or on any maps."

I spelled it for him.

"Good," he said. "There's this one sign I'm proud of. *Where Do You Stand on the Modonoland Question?* I love it. Randy's personal answer is *On My Head.* Mine is *Abashed.*"

"I like that."

"I thought you might. I'm sorry to call you with such a stupid question, but I figured it might be uncool to spell the country wrong. You're positive there really is such a place?"

"Positive."

"I'll take your word for it. People keep asking me where it is. So far I've been dodging the question."

"That's a good policy."

"You don't know either?"

"I used to, but I can never remember." Arlette brought over a fresh cup of coffee and I swallowed half of it. "Tell them it's near Kenya," I suggested. "Most of Africa is near Kenya."

"It is?"

"Isn't it?"

"To be honest with you, I'm not entirely certain where Kenya is."

"Well, we don't want to get hung up on geography."

"I'm hip. I'm sorry I had to call—"

"It's all right. I was wondering how you were doing. Call at six."

"Right."

I cradled the phone. *The hand that phones the cradle rules the waves. Britannia waives the rules. The hand that cradles the rock*—I couldn't even take a shower or I'd wash the dye out of my hair and the putty off my ears. *Cradle, cradle. Children are starving in Hungary and you didn't finish your cradles and bream cheese. Children are hungry in Starvaring and you didn't finish your curds and whey. Little Miss Muffet was told to go stuffet—*

"Arlette!"

"Something is wrong? Evan, what is the matter?"

I inhaled and exhaled, very slowly, very solemnly. "Nothing," I said. "I'm on edge, that's all it is." Inhale, exhale. "I have to send you out again. This time you'll have to go to the fairgrounds."

"I will go."

"You will have to find a certain man and make arrangements for later this evening."

"Who is this man?"

"I don't know. You'll have to arrange to meet with him in a certain place—"

"Where?"

"I don't know. In a certain place and at a certain time."

"When?"

"I don't know. This is terrible. Is there any more coffee?"

She peered into my eyes. I don't guess she saw much. I was still wearing the sunglasses. She said, "Evan, I think you should sleep for an hour."

"No."

"You have had very little sleep, Evan, and——"

"I'm all right. Coffee." She brought it. I drank it. "Okay," I said, ignoring the busy little rumble in the back of my head. "Okay, just let me think for a moment. All right. This is what you'll do."

I explained it to her. I guess it registered, because she repeated it all back to me, and it sounded all right when she said it. She was a little leery of leaving me all alone, though.

"I'll be all right," I said.

"At least take a nap."

"If I can. I have things to do." She went away. *And I have promises to keep*, said the rotten little voice, *and miles to go before I sleep. And I have promises to break and miles to go before I wake. And I have Thomases to peep and smiles to look before I leap. And I have——*

I went to the mirror and glowered at it. "You are probably going mad," I told my reflection aloud. "Do you realize what you're doing? You're having verbal hallucinations. That's what you're doing. Do you realize that this may mean your mind is going? And if so, the competence of your whole brilliant plan is called into question. And since you haven't told anyone what your plan is, nobody can check it to make sure it makes sense. Maybe this is an aftereffect of the pot. Maybe you're actually still lying on the floor stoned out of your bird and it's only six in the morning and none of this has happened yet. Maybe it never will. Why do you just stand there, you schmuck in the mirror? Why don't you say something? Oh, Jesus God, what would I do if you did?"

I returned to the other room, sat on the floor, and folded up my legs in the full lotus posture. I began chanting the multiplication tables, first in English, then in French, then in Spanish and Portuguese and German and Dutch and Serbo-Croat and on and on, switching from language to language, babbling inanely onward and waiting for whatever was happening to either improve or deteriorate.

Very weird it was, believe me. I was in several minds at once, one of them chanting polylingual gibberish, one punning endlessly, one terrified that I was going crazy, one not giving a damn, and one little spark of sense somewhere in the background shaking its head at all the others. *If I can just get control*, it was saying, *everything will be all right again. Let all the other fellows burn themselves out. I'm still here, fellow. I'll take care of you.*

16

We left Arlette's place at a quarter to seven. I sat beside her in the little Renault. She drove. She had suggested that I might huddle on the floor of the back seat, but there wasn't room, and I had the feeling that it might provoke comment if someone saw me doing that. It felt odd being outside in daylight. I wasn't especially nervous about it, though, until Arlette advised me to be calm. "Because if you perspire, the putty will run from your nose and ears," she said.

I wished she hadn't mentioned it. Trying not to perspire is the surest way to do it. I didn't let it bother me, though, nor did I say anything. Talking wasn't much fun anymore.

Just before we left the apartment, I put the finishing touches to my disguise, lodging little gobs of cotton batten between my lips and teeth. This was supposed to change the shape of my mouth. I don't know if it looked different, but it certainly felt different.

While Arlette contended with the traffic, I made sure we hadn't forgotten anything. The heroin was in my clothes, which I was wearing. The Japanese automatic was in one pocket, the spare clip in another. Arlette's false ID would go in her purse eventually, but I didn't want to give her the chance to lose it before then; it was in yet another of my pockets. She had the clear glasses in her purse. I was wearing my sunglasses and didn't really care if she lost the others. The mike and the receiving unit were locked in the trunk.

Seth and Randy had called in at six, at which time we had synchronized our watches. I told them to meet me at the Lost Children booth at Expo at 2100 hours. They didn't know what that meant—it was kind of a dumb thing to tell a draft-dodger—so I translated it as nine o'clock. They said they would be there. I said, "Give 'em hell, men," and Seth said, "Keep the faith, baby," which sums up the generation gap fairly well.

"Emile and the rest are supposed to be at their posts by seven," I told Arlette now. "Figure they'll be there by seven fifteen at the outside. We should be ready to move in almost anytime after that."

"We have time."

"Good. Nine o'clock at the fairgrounds? Is that right? The Lost and Found booth?"

"Yes."

"Just checking. I hope he'll be there."

"So do I. Evan, I am a little worried about that man. I believe he is a drunkard."

"I'm positive of it."

"Is he reliable?"

"I don't know."

"But you selected him—"

"He's crazy enough to do what I want him to do," I said. "We gain in courage what we lose in dependability."

"He was very drunk when I saw him."

"Good. That means you found the right man."

"It was difficult. I did not know his name."

"I never learned it. What is it, by the way?"

"Oh. I did not think to ask. Does it matter?"

"Probably not. Don't worry about it."

"If I knew what it was you wished him to do—"

"You told him what I would pay him?"

"Yes. He said for that money he would fly through hell on a broomstick."

"I may hold him to that."

For the rest of the ride I went over the procedure with her. She checked out all the way down the line. She wasn't a stupid girl, I decided. Not by any means. It was just unnerving to have a conversation with her, that was all.

We drove out of the city and through a wasteland of suburbs to Point X. She had no trouble finding it. The road came to within two hundred yards of the river. The terrain between the two was hilly, with a lot of shrubbery and deep ground cover. From the road we could just make out the crest of the hill where Claude would be poised with his rifle and binoculars.

I walked part of the way through the field, my ears cocked, putty and all. I stopped when I heard conversation. Claude's voice, then Jean Berton's. They had arrived at Point X, then. Soon the Bertons would move off to their spot and set up the machine gun in the brush clump.

I checked my watch. We were early. I went back to the car and told Arlette to head back to the gas station we had passed half a mile back. We had time to spare, and I figured that every smoke screen we could create would do us that much more good. I took a fistful of dimes into the outdoor phone booth and spent every last one of them on terrifying phone calls. I called the British Consulate and told them there was a bomb in the basement. I called three different police stations and reported crimes ranging from armed robbery to murder. I turned in a variety of false fire alarms. I threw bomb scares at several downtown movie houses, advising them to clear the building and call the police. I behaved, in short, in a thoroughly antisocial manner. By the time I was through, someone could have called in to announce the imminent assassination of the Queen and no one would have paid the slightest attention to him. They would just write it off as another message from the Telephone Maniac.

When the dimes ran out, I got back into the car. Arlette returned to Point X, drove a little way down the road, and found a sheltered spot to park the Renault. She left her purse in the car. I thought about locking my jacket in the trunk and decided I would rather have it with me.

We walked a short way into the field together, then separated. Arlette cut over toward the machine gun site while I headed for Claude and his rifle. I walked very slowly, very carefully. It didn't matter too very much if Jean and Jacques heard Arlette coming; she would ostensibly be bringing them a message in a hurry, not sneaking up on them. But my approach to Claude was something else. I was disguised, and if he spotted me, he might very well shoot me.

So I took my time, moving slowly closer to the great rise of ground. Halfway to the top I stopped to check my watch. I had 7:24. The target ship was due in sixteen minutes and might appear almost anytime before then. Or after then, for that matter.

Shoes were now a liability. So was the jacket. I took them off and placed them where I hoped I would find them again. I transferred the spare clip to a pants pocket and clutched the Marley in my hand.

Onward and upward. By now, I thought, Arlette was talking with the Bertons. She would tell them that there had been a last-minute switch. The Queen's barge was running ahead of schedule, the royal trappings and the Queen herself were out of sight in the hold, and a variety of precautions had been taken because of assassination rumors. She would explain that Claude had a description of the remodeled barge and would take appropriate action. So they must be ready for Claude's trio of shots at any moment.

I hoped that would do it. There was no way to pass on the spurious information to Emile. I could only trust him to go along with the majority. Once triangulated gunfire rained on the target vehicle, he would have to believe that it was the right ship and go through with his own role.

I drew closer, and worked my way around a stand of aspen, and saw Claude.

He might have been carved in stone. He sat on his haunches at the very peak of the rise, a high-powered rifle across his knees, one hand on the stock, the other hand holding a pair of binoculars to his eyes. I stood motionless watching him, and he didn't move any more than I did. I watched that coldhearted, sadistic son of a bitch, and an unaccountable lump rose in my throat. When Québec was free, I thought, when the MNQ achieved its goal, there could be a statue of him posed thus in downtown Montreal. Claude, with binoculars and rifle, prepared to sacrifice himself for *Québec Libre*.

I inched closer, a cautious step at a time. I couldn't avoid a great wave of guilt. Who was I to mess up their show? Who was I, for that matter, to play God? Here were four men with a mission, and I was about to wreck it for them. And wreck them in the bargain. Emile, who, while mad remained a sweet and gentle man. Jean and Jacques, a fairly bloody pair of killers but somehow charming just the same. And Claude—but Claude, fortunately, was a man for whom I could not summon up a whit of sympathy.

It was a good thing he was the one on the hill. Otherwise I'm not sure I could have gone through with it.

I took a breath, moved in as close as I dared, then looked beyond Claude at the river below.

And discovered that my plan had a hole in it.

I couldn't have anticipated the flaw. It was necessary to stand in that spot to know what was wrong, and I'd ruled out an afternoon reconnaissance mission as too risky and time-consuming. But now I was right there at Point X and I could see that the script wouldn't play as written.

I had intended to stay behind Claude until the target ship came into view. Then, as it approached the right spot, I would rush him. If possible I'd club him over the head with my pistol and fire three signal shots with his rifle. If I couldn't get to him in time, I'd still fire three shots, but I'd use the pistol to do it, and at least one of the bullets would wind up in Claude. Hopefully.

It seemed like a hell of a fine idea at the time. But what I hadn't known was that I couldn't see enough of the river from where I stood. The target ship could cruise right on by without my even knowing it. And if I tried to get any closer, Claude would smell me.

Don't sweat, I told myself. Or the putty will run—

The pang of conscience returned, supported now by a basis of logic. Call it fate, I thought. This is the way things were meant to be. Go home and contemplate your navel—

No. They wanted to strike a blow for Free Québec and they had that right. They wanted to commit the grand act. They wanted to die as martyrs. So be it.

But how? I could rush him as planned, and if I got to him in time to knock him bowlegged, it would be all right. But if I didn't—and I couldn't expect to—then I would have to shoot him. And if I fired a shot before the ship was in place, everything would come unglued.

And if I didn't get him clubbed senseless before he turned on me, and if I didn't shoot him either but tried to take him without shooting, I knew what would happen.

He would beat the living crap out of me.

I took one more step toward him, and looked at my watch, and took a breath, and gripped the automatic by the barrel.

I said, *"Claude, you fool!"*

He whirled to face me, dropping first the binoculars and then the rifle. "But who . . . oh, it is you . . . but what are you doing . . . but . . ."

I strode toward him, fury in my face, scorn in my voice. "Fool, dolt, pig! Have you no eyes? Do you sleep at such a moment?"

"What are you talking about?"

"The royal barge, you ass! While true patriots man their posts, you allow it to sail on past us all! You fail to fire the signal shots!"

I was right beside him now. He towered over me, but when my words sank in, his jaw dropped almost to the level of mine. "But it cannot be," he stammered. "Never did I cease to watch the river. I swear it! On the grave of my aunt I—"

"Use your eyes, fool! There!"

"I cannot—"

"Then, pick up the field glasses, oaf. Look and see for yourself!"

He bent down to pick up the glasses, and I squeezed that gun by the barrel and hit him harder than I had ever hit anything before in my life. I put everything into the blow, and if it hadn't done the job, I could have jumped right into the river. The gun bounced off his head and out of my hand, and I felt the force of the impact clear up my arm to the shoulder. He went down like the *Titanic*.

Then for a moment or two I was frozen, quite immobile. I managed ultimately to retrieve my pistol and stuff it into my belt. I rolled Claude aside and positioned myself in his vantage point, rifle across my knees, binoculars to my eyes. I scanned the river, wondering if the barge could already have passed us.

My watch said 7:33. I couldn't believe that only nine minutes had gone by since I looked at it last, and I checked it to make sure it hadn't stopped. It was still running. *Ticking like a watch. Talking like a witch. Walking like—*

My mind was still playing games with me. I got hold of myself and concentrated on the river. I had recovered from my bout with lunacy while Arlette was visiting the Expo site, and I had managed to stay on top of things since then. I couldn't let go now.

I kept taking quick glances at my watch. Time seemed to rush by and creep along all at once. It took forever for a minute to go by, but every time one passed without the appearance of the barge, we came closer and closer to failure.

How long could I count on Seth and Randy's delaying action? By now the royal barge had almost certainly entered the narrows. If they had begun their demonstration, how long could they keep it up before the police hauled them all off to jail? I had asked for a minimum of fifteen minutes and a cushion of half an hour, and it was conceivable that fifteen minutes was too much to expect, and it was equally conceivable that the barge would be running a bit ahead of schedule when they tried to block its passage.

Which meant that it might reach Point X by eight o'clock, or even a few minutes before. I could do nothing, trusting in Emile and the Bertons to wait for Claude's shot. But suppose they spotted the barge themselves? Suppose one of them came to check on Claude? And in any case, what was Arlette going to do? And what of the grand act, the justification of everybody's martyrdom?

If the target ship didn't come into sight by ten minutes of eight, I decided I was going to have to forget about it. It might have passed us already, it might have been delayed, it could even get caught in the Modonoland demonstration along with Mrs. Battenberg.

If the target ship didn't show by then, I would wing three shots at the first goddam boat that came along, whatever the hell it was. A cabin cruiser, an ocean liner, a kayak, anything.

It was getting darker. I took off my sunglasses, then raised the binoculars once more. One hand on them, one on the rifle butt.

Time rushed and crawled.

There was no mistaking the target ship. It came into view at 7:43, seven minutes short of my chosen zero hour. It was long and broad and flat, with a Canadian flag at the bow and flags of all the provinces spaced out along either side. I had trouble believing that anything could move that slowly. I put down the glasses and raised the rifle, tucking the butt into my shoulder. It was hell holding off, but I waited until it drew up past me and reached the designated spot, halfway between me and the Bertons and directly opposite from Emile.

Then I squeezed the trigger three times.

I'm pretty sure I missed. Almost immediately upon the report of my third shot came the chatter of the Berton machine gun off to the left, and I saw bullets churn the water in front of the ship and plow into the bow and port side. I kept firing, too. I didn't bother aiming. I just wanted to make enough of a racket so that Emile couldn't help get the point.

Now, now—

He got a late start. I suppose he had already seen the barge and discounted it as other than the one he was waiting for. So he probably didn't have his engine ready when our shots rang out. I got as close to the edge of the cliff as I could and looked down, but I couldn't see him at all. I listened for the sound of his engines. All I could hear was the machine gun. I looked at the barge—it had not stopped but was pressing forward on its course.

I emptied my rifle at it.

And then I saw him in the stern of his little boat, bent over the engine, running dead on target at full speed. He was magnificent. For a moment I thought he was going to pass them on his port side, but he saw the error himself and corrected it in plenty of time. I watched him, and I listened to the machine gun, and I saw him turn from the engine to check his fuses and timers. At the very last moment, just a second or two before impact, he stood up in the boat like Washington crossing the Delaware. He turned toward the bank and took off his hat and hurled it into the air.

And his boat rammed the barge.

There was a noise of the sort the earth will make if it ever cracks in the middle. Both boats absolutely disintegrated in a dizzying shower of light and sound. The sky, a moment ago the dull charcoal gray of twilight, was putting on an incredible color show. Reds and blues and whites and yellows and greens shot everywhere, everywhere. Skyrockets, roman candles, pinwheels. All the fireworks intended for the Confederation Centennial Celebration had gone off at once, backed up by a boatful of dynamite and plastique.

I think the machine gun stopped. If it was still going, then the cacophony of the fireworks were drowning it out. Explosion followed explosion, colors burst in the air like meteor showers.

And someone was leaping up and down, tears in his eyes, shaking his fist at the heavens, pounding his feet on the ground, shrieking *"Québec Libre!"* over and over at the top of his lungs.

Me.

17

I ran through brush and tall grass, heading for the machine gun site. I had my shoes on again, and my lumpy jacket, and I plunged through the ground cover with elephantine grace. The Marley automatic was in my right hand. A pocket contained the revolver Claude had been carrying. I raced down the side of the hill, broke through a patch of open ground, and kept going.

I shouted, "Jean! Jacques! Are you all right?"

They leaped out from a clump of brush, and for a bad moment I froze, the weight of the Marley so great suddenly that I could barely hold onto it. In my mind I raised the gun and dropped them with two quick shots—

"Evan, comrade! Did you see it? Did you hear it? What a blow for Québec, my brother!"

One of them was gripping me by the shoulders, lifting me into the air. The other danced like an Indian in war paint, whooping and cheering, filling the air with a combination of OAS and Québeçois oaths. I let go of the gun, delighted that I was not going to need it now.

"So they try to trick us," Jacques roared. "A disguised vessel, a change in schedule. They think this will outwit us?" He pounded his fists against his thighs. "And the fireworks! Never in my existence have I seen such a display. Fireworks for the Centennial? No, not now. Fireworks that accompanied England's Queen to hell. Fireworks to tell the Devil to open the gates for her!"

We all shouted and danced and sang, all four of us. Arlette had come out of hiding. We embraced one another and talked of the heroism of Emile and the glory of French Canada. The brothers did not seem to have the slightest doubt that they had hit the right boat and had obtained the desired effect, with the added and unexpected bonus of the fireworks. So I did not have to make martyrs of them, and that was all to the good, because I am not sure I could have done it. They were no threat to us now, though. And, when they did eventually find out that the Queen had not been on the boat, they would probably fail to blame me for it. At any rate, I intended to be out of the country by then.

"And Claude," said Jacques. "Where is the grim and brooding and valiant specter of Claude?"

I sighed. "You did not hear him?"

"The shots, of course."

"The scream."

"But no. He screamed?"

"When he fell from the cliff, " I said mournfully. "Carried away by an excess of patriotic enthusiasm, our friend Claude lost his footing and plunged to the rocks below." I sighed, partly for effect, partly at the memory of his weight as I dragged him to the edge and sent him on his way. "He must have died instantly," I said. "I'm sure he did not feel a thing."

"Alas, for our comrade Claude," Jean said.

"I never liked him," Jacques said thoughtfully.

"Who could like him? An odious creature, no? But he died a hero's death."

I took Arlette's hand. "We must go now," I said. "You two will return to the city?"

They exchanged glances. "But no, Evan. Since we have thus far avoided martyrdom, we thought to further prolong our lives. We have reservations on a flight to Mexico in just a few hours."

"It is sad that we must leave Canada," Jean said.

"But it would be sadder to die here. There will come a day when we return. And there are always other fights to be fought in other lands." Jacques embraced me. "Believe me, my comrade, you will hear more of us."

I could believe it.

They offered us a lift, but I said we had a car of our own nearby. The boys kissed me on both cheeks and bussed Arlette lingeringly upon the mouth, and then they went one way and we went the other, in a hurry.

I closed my eyes and took a mental picture of my little list. *Minna, assassination, heroin, cops.* I took a mental eraser and carefully rubbed out *assassination.*

Minna, heroin, cops—

Arlette found a way to get onto the new superhighway that led to Expo without going through much of Montreal. This turned out to be an extremely wise move because, from all indications, the city was in a state of utter chaos. Between my lunatic phone calls, the demonstration at the narrows, and the unscheduled fireworks display, every police and fire siren in the city was raising thirty kinds of hell. The traffic must have been unbelievable. We hit some slow stretches ourselves, but it wasn't bad.

I had been afraid that Arlette would ask questions that I wouldn't much want to answer. Questions about my role in Claude's diving act, which I wanted to talk about even less than I wanted to think about, or questions about what we would do when we got to the fairgrounds, which I wanted to tell her at the last minute. But she surprised me. She chattered incessantly about the destruction of the barge, the nerveless manner in which Jean and Jacques had raked the craft with machine gun shells, the *élan* with which Emile had tossed his hat into the air an instant before he was disintegrated. It was a heady triumph for her. She no longer felt like a traitor; on the contrary, the display had overwhelmed her with furious patriotism.

At the fair we paid $2.50 each for one-day admissions and passed through the turnstiles. We were early, and neither the boys nor our man were at the Lost & Found booth. I had my sunglasses on again, and my cap, and I still felt frighteningly conspicuous in the crowd. I told Arlette to keep an eye on the booth and found my way to a men's room.

I checked myself in the mirror. My nose was a mess, and I had to do what I could to reshape the putty on it. The ears were still pretty good, and the dye had remained in my hair. I locked myself in a stall and waited for it to become nine o'clock. The place provided in privacy what it lacked in comfort.

At five of nine Randy's voice said, "Evan? You here?"

I emerged from my hiding place. I told him we had scored a direct hit on the fireworks barge and could put the expedition down as an unqualified success. He was quite proud of his end of things, and he had every right to be; the Modonoland demonstration had mobilized over seventy Canadian youths and had stopped the royal barge dead in its tracks for forty minutes. One girl had sprained her wrist, but that was the only casualty.

I didn't tell him about the casualties in my area of the operation. Claude, Emile, and whoever had the ill luck to be on the fireworks barge. Figuring a four-man crew, I had helped create six martyrs to the cause of Free Québec. And only two of them were voluntary ones.

"The pilot's with Seth and Arlette," Randy told me. "They're waiting for us. You ready?"

"I guess so. How do I look?"

"I wouldn't have too much trouble picking you out of a crowd."

"Oh," I said. "The hell with it. Let's go."

The helicopter pilot was standing with Seth and Arlette a few yards off to the side of the Lost & Found booth. His eyes were even more bloodshot than I remembered and his breath smelled inflammable. He had a hand resting in absentminded fashion upon Arlette's bottom, and his eyes were focused—well, aimed, anyway—at Myra Teale, who was still riding shotgun on a batch of purposely lost children. He turned to me, hiccuped, and grinned.

"We meet again," he said. "The fellow who was sick all over my little chopper. Got a haircut since, did you?"

"Uh," I said.

"The chopper's resting over that way. Shall we go to it?"

"That might be a good idea."

"Do you know, I think it would be." He slapped me heartily on the back. "You wouldn't want anyone to have too good a look at you, would you, my friend?"

"Uh."

"Leading them the devil of a chase, aren't you, Mr. Tanner? Oh, don't worry about me. The little mam'selle here said something about five hundred dollars."

"That's right."

"—and for five hundred dollars I'd fly through a forest fire on the back of a chicken hawk. You don't have to worry about me."

"I'm glad to hear that, Mr.—"

"Mr. Completely," he said, and laughed vacantly. "Missed her completely, that is, that's what we did. Your little girl, isn't it? And you want to fly over that same ridiculous building again, is that so? And hop the border to the States when you find her?"

"More or less."

"I'm your man. No doubt about it." His Canadian accent made that come out *No doat about it.*

He led and we followed. I told him that Seth and Randy and I would be flying with him in the chopper for the time being, and he assigned places to the three of us. Arlette wanted to know where she was going to sit and I told her she wasn't.

"I do not understand," she said.

I took a deep breath. I had been saving this for the last minute, because if she had time to think about it, she would not possibly go through with it.

"You're not coming with us," I told her. "You have a special job to do, You will carry this in your purse"—I tucked the false ID into her bag—"and you will fasten this in your hair"—I clipped the little microphone into her hair—"and you will go to the Cuban Pavilion and enter the dungeon. You will stand where we stood before, and when no one is looking, you will throw the switch on the end and drop through to the dungeon below."

She gaped at me. I rushed right on, not giving her a chance to interrupt. "They won't dare hurt you because they'll know you're a Canadian agent. What they'll do is panic. They'll want to get you out of there, and they'll want to do something with all the prisoners they've taken in the past little while. I'm almost positive they ship batches of them out of the country, or to some hiding place up in the north. As soon as they think the government is on to them, they'll make a run for it. They'll take you out of the dungeon and rendezvous with the other prisoners, and I'll have this"—I showed her the receiving unit—"so we can trace you in the helicopter. We'll wait until they lead us straight to Minna and the others. Then we'll rescue you and Minna, and the helicopter will get us all the hell out of there."

She bought it. Maybe the example of courage set by Emile and Claude was contagious. Maybe she was too simple to think it through and realize what a risk she was running. Maybe, as I prefer to think, she was just a very good girl. Whatever the reason, she bought it.

"When shall I go to the pavilion?"

"Right away."

"I shall do it. May I kiss you first? And the boys?" She kissed all three of us, then kissed the pilot, too. "You will hear me with this thing, is it not so? And you will rescue me?"

"Definitely."

We stayed in the helicopter with the engines off while she made her way onto the Expo Express and out to the Cuban Pavilion on the Île de Nôtre Dame. I listened to the receiver and had no trouble telling where she was. Everything came through clear as a bell. Now and then she would talk to me, and once she expressed aloud the fervent wish that she could hear me as well as speak to me, if only to assure herself that the equipment worked.

"I am at the pavilion," she said ultimately. "There is not too long a line. It should take me but a few minutes. Evan, which is the switch that I must throw? I cannot remember."

"The one on the right," I said aloud. As if she could hear me.

"As if you could answer me. It is all right. I will throw them all at once."

"Oh, God," I said. As if He were listening.

I told the pilot—damn it, I still didn't know his name—to start the engines. He did, and I leaped from my seat and grabbed his arm. "Off!" I shouted. "My God, they're noisy!"

"Can't fly without 'em, Mr. Tanner."

"But I can't hear over them." He cut them out, and I listened again to Arlette. I wondered if people had noticed that she was talking to herself. I suppose she wasn't speaking in much more than a whisper, but she came through loud and clear.

With the engines off, that is. With them on, I couldn't hear a thing. If the fool thing had come with earphones, we would have been all right, but it didn't. I told the pilot to leave the engines off until we had a particular reason to start flying. For the moment, it was more important to maintain communication with Arlette.

Seth wondered aloud how we would be able to follow her in the copter if we couldn't hear her. The same thought had already occurred to me. I said we would have to pick them up with aerial reconnaissance when they left the building and keep them under constant visual observation. Randy wanted to know if that wasn't risky. I asked him if he had a better idea, and he said he didn't. Neither did anyone else.

All we had to do was lose them. That would be the payoff, all right—we would scare them into skipping the country with all the prisoners, Minna and Arlette included. And then we would lose them, and that would be the last I would see of either of them.

Arlette's voice, just a whisper: "I am within the building. There is a guard, I must wait until he goes away. He is not looking at me now. Did you say the switch on the left? I will throw them all, now—"

Then there was a lot of noise, all at once, shouts in Spanish and English and other languages, machinery noises. And then, over it all, Arlette's voice ringing out: "In the name of J.B. Westley and the Dominion of Canada you are all under arrest! In the name—"

Halfway through the sentence some of the background noise stopped, as if the aperture leading from the dungeon to the first floor had been closed again. And then there was a sort of thunk, and Arlette stopped talking. I heard an excited babble of Cuban Spanish but couldn't make out the words.

What happened, man?"

"I think they knocked her out."

"The poor chick—"

"Shhh . . ."

I hoped they hadn't hurt her. As I saw it, she was well out of it; a bump on the head would be a small price to pay for an hour or so of unconsciousness. From our standpoint, it was both good and bad. She would be unable to tell me what was happening, but she would be equally incapable of answering any questions the Cubans might put to her.

I concentrated on the Spanish. "They're going through her purse," I said. "They found her ID card. They're reading it. I hope the lighting down there is terrible. . . . They believe the ID. One of them just told the other that she's a Canadian agent."

"Is she all right, Evan?"

"Just a minute. I think she must be coming to, because one just said they should chloroform her at once. That's good, that's damned good. She couldn't have been badly hurt, and the chloroform won't hurt her now. It'll just keep her out. If she were awake now, she'd be terrified—"

"Do you blame her?"

"No, not a bit. This way she'll sleep. Oh, hell!"

"What?"

"They found the bug in her hair. Damn it, they know what it is. I wonder if—"

A loud, ear-splitting noise came through the receiver, followed by absolute silence.

"They smashed it," I announced. I tossed the useless receiver to the floor of the copter. "They smashed the hell out of it. Better start the engines. There's nothing to listen to anyway, not now. And we ought to get over toward the Cuban place right away." I swallowed. "They'll probably wait until the fair closes before they move her. But what if they don't? If they move out before we get into position . . ."

The prop spun, the engines caught. They drowned out the rest of my sentence, but that didn't matter. Everyone knew the ending.

18

As our pilot pointed out, it wouldn't be fitting to hover permanently in the air over the Cuban Pavilion. Helicopters buzzing to and fro were a common enough sight at Expo, but helicopters on stakeout duty might draw stares. We worked out a pattern of lazy, looping circles, dipping here, rising there, but contriving to keep the Cuban building constantly in view. Our pilot came up with a small pair of binoculars, and I kept them trained on the pavilion as well as I could. I wished I had thought to bring Claude's field glasses along. These were less powerful and spotlighted a smaller field.

The pilot was giving us a surprisingly smooth flight, and I found myself almost relaxed. From time to time the memory of our near miss of the British Pavilion would set my nerves on end, but by and large the ride was far less harrowing than thoughts of what would happen if we missed them.

This watching and waiting was a pain in the ass. It seemed I'd been doing a lot of it lately. Sitting endlessly around the apartment while Arlette ran errands, crouching interminably on the crest of the hill waiting for the fireworks barge, and now circling eternally around the Cuban Pavilion waiting for—

Waiting for what? For a whole lot of people to leave it, and to do so in a secretive manner.

The pilot began shouting something. I couldn't understand him at first, then realized he was offering me a drink. I wondered how it might affect me. The little voice in my head still blurted out some fool thing every once in a while, and I didn't know whether liquor would oil its tongue or rust it. I decided to find out and accepted the bottle of McNaughton's, tilted it, and let a gratifying quantity leap straight for my liver. The pilot gestured at the boys and I passed the bottle their way. When they sent it back, I returned it to the pilot and watched him pour an impossible amount down his throat. He didn't even swallow, just tucked in his glottis and poured it down the pipe.

I said something about drinking and flying. "Don't give it a second thought," he said, and hiccuped. "Any bloody fool can fly this crate with his eyes closed. Want to try your hand at it?"

"I don't think so."

"Oh, come on, give it a try. I'll show you what to do."

"I'd better keep an eye down below."

"How about you boys, then?" They came forward, and he had Seth sit at the controls while he and Randy watched over his shoulders. "A good skill for any man to know. Especially for you boys. Americans, are you? Now when you get over to Vietnam, you can be helicopter pilots. It's the key weapon of the war, do you know. One lad at the controls like so, and another on the side potting away at the wogs with a tommy gun, and one more man to send the naphtha on its way. Pay attention while I teach you now, and they'll make officers of you."

While the fair itself didn't close until the small hours of the morning, most of the national pavilions began shutting down a few hours earlier. At 11:15 the doors of the Cuban Pavilion were closed. Not long afterward the lights went out—one by one, though, not all at once, as they must have when Arlette hit the switches.

"Won't be long now," I said. "There goes the building across the street from them. As soon as a few more shut down, it will be safe for them to start moving prisoners."

"Good thing, too. We're running a shade low."

"We're running out of fuel?"

"No, not that. Or yes, in a manner of speaking." He held up the bottle of McNaughton's. It was not the original bottle—that had plummeted into the canal after we'd emptied it. This was the second bottle, and not too much whiskey remained in it.

There had been a great deal of whiskey swallowed, and not all of it by our nameless captain. Not by any means. We all of us had achieved a precarious balance somewhere between happiness and sobriety, and with the alcohol working in our bloodstreams we had turned into rather a cheery little group. The four of us careened drunkenly through the summer skies, Seth and Randy leading us in such traditional pacifist anthems as "Halls of Montezuma" and "Those Caissons Go Rolling Along." The pilot contributed "It's a Long Way to Tipperary," and I sang "If You Don't Like Your Uncle Sammy Go Back to Your Home

'Cross The Sea."

By this time we had all had a turn at piloting the copter. Of the four of us, I guess I was the worst at it. He was right, though; it was an extremely easy machine to manage, and it certainly did seem as though one could handle it better drunk than sober.

Randy was warbling "I Don't Want To Be a Soldier, I Don't Want to Go to War," and doing so in a lamentably inadequate Cockney accent, when I saw something through the glasses and motioned at him to shut up. Several dark cars had drawn up at the rear entrance of the Cuban building. I shouted to the pilot to take us in for a closer look. There were four cars, identical black sedans with what looked like some sort of crest painted on the front doors.

"That's how they move them, "I said. "Consulate cars. They even have diplomatic immunity going for them."

We flew in a straight line, moving as far off from the building as possible while still keeping the cars in sight. I saw the doors open and told the pilot to move in closer again. A dozen people emerged from the building and entered the cars. Two men seemed to be carrying something heavy, something that looked as though it might be Arlette.

The car doors slammed shut and the cars moved out from the curb.

"Now we follow 'em, Mr. Tanner?"

"Right."

"And no problem, that. Easier at night than in the daytime. With their headlights glowing, they look like a pack of fireflies now, don't they?"

"What do we look like?"

"Could you let me have that again, sir?"

"We've lights of our own," I said. "And with all due respect, this thing does make a hell of a racket. It's one thing to fly back and forth over the fairgrounds. There are always helicopters doing that, and one looks like the next. But in downtown Montreal—"

"Then you think they'll"—*burp*—"head for the city, eh?"

"The city or the open road. Either way we'll be pretty obvious in our pursuit, won't we?"

He swung around to grin at me, showing more teeth than most families have under one roof. I still hadn't entirely gotten accustomed to the idea that he could fly the thing without seeing where he was going. "I could turn our lights off," he said.

"That doesn't sound like a good idea."

"'Tisn't, but I could. Still, the noise is worse than the lights, wouldn't you say? But there are tricks to every trade, don't you know, and I can keep on a course with them and not let them know about it. Used to fly highway patrol out in Ontario"—*burp*—"bouncing radar at the bleeders. It was a rare one saw me quick enough to slow down. I'll follow these Cuban rascals as sure as my name is—now what in the devil!"

So I didn't found out his name then, either. "Something's wrong?"

"Lost 'em for a minute," he said. I winced; we hadn't even left the fairgrounds yet. "But there they are, four glowworms on parade. Can't let that happen again, can we, now?"

A little while later I had to admit that he knew what he was doing. His trailing method amounted to guessing where the cars were going next, dropping back out of sight, then circling on ahead and getting there ahead of them. It wasn't even necessary to keep them constantly in sight, just so long as we were able to guess where they would go next.

In built-up areas this still amounted to fairly close pursuit, since the motorcade might turn off onto another route at any time. We were still out of their sight almost all the time, and the generally high noise level in those sections, plus the screening effect of buildings, kept us concealed. The cars worked their way around the city and struck out northeastward. Once they hit open country, they were easier to follow than a juggler on the Orpheum Circuit. There was one main road and they stayed on it for miles. We would lay doggo behind them, make a wide sweep to the left or the right, hover until they came into view, then cut off to the side again. There was always the chance that they would pick up a side road, but our fearless leader assured us he could locate them easily enough if they did. The branch routes were few and far between, and the Cuban convoy, four identical cars doing a steady sixty-plus miles per hour and spaced five car lengths apart, would be virtually impossible to miss on a lightly traveled minor highway. Especially at night, with their lights visible miles away.

As it turned out, we didn't even have to play hide-and-seek. We were in full view of them when they made their turn onto a narrow dirt road curving off to the northwest.

"And now we'd best play 'em a trifle tighter," said our hero. "Pass the bloody bottle, eh?" Glug, glug; *burp.* "'K you. Don't want to let 'em out of sight. That's not a road they'd take to get to another road. They'll be stopping somewhere along it, and once their lights are out on a road like that, we'd have not a chance of finding 'em. I'll keep us about this far to the rear of 'em and . . . there, we'll fly without lights. Been giving me a touch of a headache anyway. I shouldn't think they'll hear us at this distance. Keep the glasses on them, why don't you? Once they cut their lights, it'll be as though the earth swallowed them alive, and you'll want to have the spot pinpointed."

I nodded, watched the last car's taillights through the binoculars. I wondered where the hell they were going. Before they skirted the city, I would have guessed they'd head straight for the Cuban consulate. Instead they were off in the woods, out in the middle of nowhere.

"I say, Tanner? What do you do when they go to ground?"

"Rescue Arlette and Minna, that's the little girl, and get out of the country in a hurry. This thing'll hold two more passengers, won't it? The girl's very tiny, she can ride in my lap."

"The other can ride in mine," he said, chortling. "How do you mean, rescue them?"

"When you go fishing, what do you use for bait?"

"Depends what's in the water."

"Uh-huh. What we do depends on what kind of setup they've got. I can't tell until I see it."

"Got a bit of firepower, have you?"

"Two pistols." I had two seven-shot clips for the Marley. Claude's revolver was a snub-barreled .38 with five shells in it. The chamber under the hammer was empty. We had nineteen shots, which didn't constitute much under the heading of firepower.

"Handguns," he said. "Look in the gearbox there and you'll find a third one. About as accurate as spitting on a windy day, but hit a chap in the finger with it, and it'll take his whole arm off." I believed that when I saw the gun, a .44 Magnum with a muzzle hole big enough to walk through. "And take the shooter's arm off with the recoil," he went on. "Won it off a trapper up near Keewatin playing high, low, jack, and the game. Then, wouldn't you know he'd have to insist on another game, staking this little Eskimo girl of his against the gun. Lost her to me and hadn't a thing left to wager for her, and don't you know he tried to welsh on the bet. No offense, by the way. I'm a fourth Welsh myself on my mother's side." Glug, glug. "So here I was with a gun I'd not owned for more than half an hour, and what could I do but blow his brains out with it? Never shot the ruddy thing since. That Eskimo girl"—*burp*—"the smell of her was enough to curdle reindeer milk, but warm as a fire on a cold night." He smiled fondly at the memory. "But that's three guns instead of two, for what small good it does. You'd do well to have a tommy gun."

"I know." If only there had been a way to bring along the Bertons' machine gun.

"Still, when they don't know you're coming, they won't have the table set, will they now? The old element of surprise. Sneak in fast and spirit out the woman and Devil take the hindmost. Then you'll want me to put you over the border, eh? Would it do to set you down just over the Vermont line?"

"I think so. Will you have enough fuel?"

"Might or might not. Could be close, but if it runs tight, we'll just set her down somewhere and fill up with gasoline. Silly thing doesn't fuss about fuel. Would run on rock salt if you could get it to burn. Whoa, now, where have they gone to? Did you spot it?"

"Yes," I pointed. "They swung left just past those trees and cut the lights."

"Got it. Got the spot fixed firm enough and won't forget it. Off we go."

He took us around to the right, explaining that he would give them time to leave their cars and go wherever they were going before coming in tight for an aerial survey. We sailed off to the right, spun lazily around, and headed back. I had already lost my bearings, but he seemed to remember the spot I'd pointed to. He brought us down low and let the copter skim over the tops of the trees. For a while we saw nothing but trees. Then the trees came to an abrupt halt and we were out over a long, flat clearing. I made out the four cars, a truck, a long low building of concrete block with a flat roof.

"Well, now," he said suddenly. "A flock of cars is one thing, but you can't expect a little egg crate like this to trail one of those."

I didn't understand at first. I thought he meant the truck, and wondered if he might be making a joke, and if I perhaps ought to laugh at it.

Then I looked out at the clearing and got the joke but didn't laugh. Because it wasn't just a clearing. It was an airstrip, and there was one hell of a big silvery jetliner perched on it.

"Now in this particular sort of water," said the Jolly Aviator, "I don't know that I'd use bait at all. I think I'd drop some dynamite and see what came to the surface."

"Shhh."

"Did you see the size of that bird, though? You could put the chopper in its luggage compartment."

"Shhhh."

We had landed the chopper about a quarter of a mile from the landing strip, and now we were walking back along the dirt road in a reasonable facsimile of silence. Arlette's entrance had shaken them up, all right. Unless I was very far off the mark, they were about to fill up the plane with all the people they had snatched and beat it out of the country in a hurry. If we didn't do something, Arlette and Minna would be spending the rest of August in Havana.

It wasn't surprising that they were shook up. Arlette and I had dropped in on them once when nobody was home, and whatever traces we had left behind was enough to put four men on guard duty all night. Arlette's second visit, combined with the general hysteria we had created throughout Montreal, must have nudged them over the edge. They wouldn't be kidnapping anybody else now. They'd just put the last load of prisoners on the plane and send all the evidence home to Fidel.

"We've got three guns," I told them. "Mr. . . . uh, the captain here, he'll use his own. I'll hang onto the thirty-eight. That leaves one of you fellows for the thirty-two automatic. It's the lightest of the lot. Have either of you had any experience with handguns?" They hadn't. "Well, which of you is best with a rifle? Who's done the most shooting?"

Neither of them had done any shooting. Seth remembered that he had been fair with an air rifle at a shooting gallery on Times Square some years back. That put him one up on Randy and earned him the gun.

"There's a lot to be said for basic training," I told them. "If only there was a way you could do your eight weeks and then cop out—"

"They don't approve of that," Randy said.

"They call it desertion," Seth said, "and frown on it."

"It's a shame. Maybe you won't have to shoot anybody. If you do, just point the gun at the person you want to shoot. And squeeze the trigger. If you jerk it, you'll hit something else. Here—"I took the clip out and showed him how to aim and fire while we walked along.

Randy, the unarmed one, must have read Mao's book on guerrilla warfare. He bent over from time to time, picking up throwing-size stones and filling his pockets with them. He also got hold of a stick about five feet long, which he said would be useful for hitting people over the head. All in all, I figured he would be capable of doing more damage to the enemy than Seth, and perhaps as much as the rest of us, too.

We walked a little farther, and I put my finger to my lips, then motioned to the others to follow me in the rest of the way at twenty-yard intervals. We would make less noise that way. I picked out a cluster of trees on the perimeter of the landing strip, some thirty yards from the plane, perhaps twice that distance from the concrete-block structure. I crouched there in the shadows and waited until they joined me one by one.

I watched the plane and the building. The aircraft, as far as I could tell, was empty now. There were guards flanking the doorway of the building and three more guards, rifles slung across their shoulders, were smoking cigars down at the far end. I had no idea who was inside the building or what was going on there. It had no windows.

The guards were a far cry from the ones who had done duty at the pavilion. These were old line *barbuda* types, with full Fidelista beards and loose-fitting khaki fatigues. There was something extremely effective about those uniforms. The men gave off an aura of insolent competence, and I matched the four of us against the five of them, balanced our three guns (and one stick, and a few rocks) against their five rifles, and I hoped Minna would enjoy Havana. It would be hot as hell this time of the year, and they wouldn't be likely to have air-conditioning, but the winters would be mild and pleasant and—

My mind was starting to do that again. I shook my head, hoping the motion might rearrange some of the cells. There had to be a way. If we could get the jump on one or two of the guards, that would make a big difference. We would have the use of their rifles and lower the odds against us. Arlette could call to them, coax them aside with the promise of sexual delight—

Not very likely. Arlette was inside the goddamned building.

I took a deep breath and plunged right back in again. One way or another, we could split up the guards and bump two of them. Then, armed with their rifles and our own pistols, and shooting from ambush, we could probably gun down the other three.

Then what?

Then we would have the building under siege, for whatever good that might do. With our guns pointing at the only door of a windowless building, we would at least be in a strong bargaining position. We couldn't get in, but they couldn't get out, and it would be to their obvious advantage to work a deal. At the very least, we could get them to release Minna and Arlette to us, and we could disable the truck and the cars so that they couldn't come after us. We could even take one of the cars—that would be part of the terms of the deal—and we'd wreck the others and leave the one where the helicopter was parked.

I went on figuring out other minor details because they were more easily resolved than the major one—namely—getting to the first two guards to start the game. Or did we really have to do it in stages? We did have three guns, and we were hidden and they were in the open, and—

And we were sixty yards away from them. I wasn't sure the .32 would *carry* thirty yards, not to mention accuracy. And I knew the Magnum, with all its power, could barely be sure of hitting the building, let alone the guard in front of it. The .38 came closest to what we needed, and if only it had a longer barrel, it might have been accurate enough for plinking at people sixty yards away. In someone else's hands, that is. Not mine.

Then how—

Ah, I thought. Forget the guards on the door, because one couldn't possibly sneak up on them. But how about the three at the far end of the building? They were goofing off, and they were within easy pistol range of what looked like fairly thick woods. We could get to them. It wasn't easy, but it was feasible. We would have to stay in the woods and work our way all around the perimeter of the landing strip. A long walk, but we would have good cover all the way and for a large part of the trek we would be out of hearing range.

Then three quick shots, or as many as it took to dispose of the three loafers. We would be in the dark while the other two guards would be outlined against the walls of the building.

I liked the odds.

"Evan?" Randy was whispering into my ear. "Got anything?"

I nodded. Then the door of the building opened, and the two guards flanking it snapped to attention, and the three bearded loafers threw away their cigarettes and came forward.

"Tell me."

A short, stocky type came through the door and headed for the jet. He was wearing a flying suit, heavy boots, goggles, and a crash helmet. He was either the pilot or a man looking for a masquerade party. He crossed over to the plane and climbed a flight of steps, disappearing into its belly.

Two more bearded types followed him from the building. After them came several clean-shaven men in close-fitting khaki slacks and blouses. Guards from the pavilion, I guessed.

"The plan, Evan."

The big jet engines kicked in and the pilot began the warm-up. I tried counting the guards, but they were moving around two much. It looked, though, as if there were more guards than we had bullets. One of them came out of the building now, his left hand fastened upon the forearm of a tall man in a rumpled suit, his right arm around the man's waist. He walked the man across the clearing to the plane. The man in the suit was a Negro. At first I thought the guard was leading him that way to keep him from resisting, but when they drew closer, I saw that it wasn't that at all. The Negro trudged on like a zombie. Either they had him drugged to the eyes or else he was ninety-five percent dead.

"Evan—"

I clenched my teeth. "The plan just washed out," I said. "It went down the drain."

He passed this bit of information on to the rest of them, speaking in a thin whisper that couldn't entirely hide his nervousness. I watched the guard lead the Negro up the steps and into the midsection of the big jet. Then more guards were following him, each with a man or a woman in tow. They would tuck their passengers into the plane and turn around and go back for more.

There were about four men to each woman. There were a few children, but not many of them. All of them, men and women and children, walked in the same robot fashion, shuffling along like the living dead. All of them had wide, glassy eyes and wore rumpled clothing.

And all of them, men and women and children, were Negroes.

I sat there watching this little parade without even trying to guess what it was all about. The Cubans were stealing Negroes. Male Negroes, female Negroes, juvenile Negroes. Fidel was starting a Negro collection. He wanted

Cubans to develop a natural sense of rhythm. He—

Then they brought Arlette and, a few Negroes later, Minna. It was easy to spot them. In that company they looked positively bleached. In other respects, however, they differed not at all from the rest of the plane's passengers. Their eyes were every bit as glazed, their walk the same fumbling stumbling shuffle.

Minna—

Something happened when I saw her. I realized, for the first time since her disappearance, that deep down inside I had not expected to see her again. A part of my unconscious mind had quietly written her off as dead, even while I was rushing around searching for her. I felt this way without ever being aware of it, and now I was seeing her again, and she was alive.

There was sudden intense pressure behind my eyeballs. Then my eyes were wet, and tears spilled down my cheeks like raindrops on a windshield. I was not sobbing. I was sitting still, breathing normally, remaining quite calm while silently crying my eyes out.

My tears were still flowing when Minna disappeared into the plane. There were a few more Negroes, and then a youngish woman in a brown and white uniform. The stewardess? The idea was unlikely enough to stop the flow of tears. I saw that the woman was carrying a small black bag and decided she must be a nurse. Someone had to be giving those zombies their periodic dosages of drugs. She looked equal to the task. Her face somehow reminded me of Claude.

Of course they needed the nurse aboard the plane. Otherwise they would need a full complement of guards to keep the passengers tractable. This way they would slump in their seats all the way to Havana and—

I whirled around. I said, "The plane."

They stared at me, the three of them. I swung my head around again. The clean-shaven guards were walking toward their cars. The *barbudas* had thinned out, most of them returning to the building.

I said, "They do it themselves all the time. They get on a plane going from El Paso to Kansas City and make the pilot fly to Havana. It's about time somebody turned the tables on them."

"You mean—"

"Right. We steal the plane."

"How?"

"All we have to do is get on it. The place is crawling with guards, but they're all staying on the ground. The airplane's got a pilot and a cargo of Negroes and that's all."

"And that hatchet-faced bitch."

"But no guards."

"One or two may have stayed aboard—"

"I don't think so, but so what? One or two we can handle. Once we're inside, what can the yoyos on the ground do? Shoot us down?"

I looked at them, Randy and Seth and Baron von Richthoften. They were nodding in agreement. For my part, I wasn't sure it would work out the way I told it.

Nor did I care. All we had to do was get on that plane. That was the only thing that mattered. Once we were aboard, I didn't care if we got jumped by eight guards and an orangutan. Because all they could do was take us along to Havana, and if Minna and Arlette were going there, I wanted to go with them. As long as we were all together, we had a chance.

I kept this to myself, by no means convinced that the others would see it my way. I watched the plane and I watched the guards, waiting for the right moment. We had to time things so that we made our move at the last possible moment, just before they closed up the belly of the aircraft.

"Get ready to jump the minute I do," I said. "I'll lead, then Seth, then Randy, and you bring up the rear. Shoot anything that gets in the way. Any questions?"

There weren't any, thank God. I kept waiting for the magic moment when all the guards would be gone. It looked as though that moment would occur a few minutes after takeoff. I braced my feet under me and got a good grip on the pistol.

I said, "Now!"

I could paint a more vivid picture of our charge across the field and up the steps and into the plane if I had been watching it from the sidelines instead of leading it. As it was, I had no real way of knowing what happened. There was some shouting. There were some gunshots—mostly ours, I think, and as far as I know, none of them hit anything. I fired the Marley three times and wasn't even aiming at anything in particular. That's what there was, shouting and shooting and running and climbing, all stuffed into a very brief segment of time.

And it worked.

They could not have been less prepared for us. I think a flash flood would have come as less of a surprise to them.

There we were, blitzing their pretty plane, and there they were, standing around like morons with their rifles hanging around their necks. By the time they knew what was happening, it had already happened.

There were two guards on the plane, bearded ones, but they were even less prepared than the ones on the ground. They had holstered revolvers, and the flaps of the holsters were buttoned down, and they couldn't unbutton them because they had their seat belts fastened. I didn't even bother with them. While they struggled with their belts I hurried forward to the pilot's cabin. Seth and Randy took care of the guards, bopping them upon the head, Seth with a pistol butt, Randy with his stick. I slowed down long enough to knocked the nurse's head against the side of the cabin.

Captain Courageous was kneeling in the entranceway, using the big Magnum to discourage guards from climbing in after us. I burst in upon the little pilot. I knew I couldn't hit him. He was so profoundly insulated he never would have felt it.

"*Qué pasa?*" he demanded.

In rapid-fire Spanish I said, "Comrade, the imperialist police are upon us. For God's sake close up the door! Throw the switch!"

He leaned forward, grabbed a lever, and tugged it. It stuck. He looked up at me and said, "But who are you? You are not—"

At least he had found the switch for me. I tugged it hard and it moved. I heard the steps draw up behind me, heard the flap slam shut. He was still babbling away and he didn't shut up until I stuck the muzzle of the gun in his face, at which point he became very, very quiet.

I said, "You are to fly to Havana?" He nodded. "No," I continued, "I believe there will be a change in plans. You will not fly to Havana. You will fly to . . ."

To where? The States? We could have crossed the border in the helicopter, but if we landed this silver bird at a jet-port, crowds would gather. And that wasn't good. Seth and Randy would spend five years in Leavenworth and I would go on trial for kidnapping. And possession of an awful lot of heroin.

Where, then? Some other part of Canada? Hardly that. If the Canadians ever got their hands on me, there wouldn't be enough left of me to bury. They would have to fill up the coffin with Arlette, who would certainly be sought in connection with the MNQ assault.

I turned to see the helicopter pilot enter the cabin, smiling like Ironjaw in the old comic strip. The plane was surrounded, he told me, and the guards were all pointing their rifles at us, but no one was shooting yet. The hatch was locked up tight and nobody could get in, the guards were out colder than Kelsey's cojones, and the nurse had fainted.

I nodded, barely paying attention. Mexico? South America? There were countries down there on sufficiently bad terms with Cuba to welcome us, but I had a feeling they were also on sufficiently good terms with the U.S.A. to extradite us in nothing flat.

Europe, then. But could the plane get us that far? Maybe. And where in Europe? The nearest point, obviously. Iceland? They had one of the few European languages I didn't trust myself in, and—

Of course.

"You will fly us directly to Shannon Airport," I told the bug-eyed pilot. "That's in Ireland, the west coast of Ireland."

"But I know only to fly to Havana!"

"So you'll learn something new. You'll fly across the ocean—"

"It is impossible!"

I let him have another long look at the gun and told him a second time what I expected of him. He opened his mouth to say something, and a strange expression flashed briefly over his face, and then he nodded. "*Sí, Señor,*" he said. "*Irlandia. Sí.*"

A hand fastened on my arm. "I couldn't make out all of that," said our Eddie Rickenbacker, "but I saw the look on his face. The bloody greaseball's going to shop us."

I translated quickly, and he nodded. "He won't fly to Ireland. He'll head out over the water and put us on course for Havana and we won't even know the difference. We'll be in some Spic airport before the bleeding sun comes up."

"We can watch him—"

"There's a hundred ways he could put it to us. And I wouldn't be quick to believe he could find Ireland if he tried. Tell him to take off his helmet."

I translated the command. The pilot, puzzled, removed his crash helmet and set it upon his knee. He asked if I wanted him to remove the goggles as well, and I passed the question on.

"Just the helmet will do," said the Flying Tiger. And he hefted his Magnum and dented the pilot's skull with it. "That's the ticket," he said, hauling the little man out of his seat. "Direct methods are best, Mr. Tanner. Now I'll fly the effing plane, and we'll be in Shannon in eight hours flat."

"You don't know how," I said.

"Ah, they're all the same. Fly one and you've flown 'em all."

"This is a jet. A large jet."

"It goes up in the air like any other."

"And comes down like snow. It's not a helicopter. It—"

"I've flown crates besides helicopters. A Piper Cub once, a Cessna—"

"This is different."

"Bigger and faster, that's the only distinction."

"Can you, uh, *find* Ireland?"

"It's east of here, isn't it? We'll go east until the ocean stops and then we'll buzz down and look for it. It's not such a small island we'd be likely to miss it."

I started to say something else, but he seemed to be ignoring me. He was fiddling with different levers, playing with the control panel. I glanced at the pilot, who was in deep slumber in the aisle. It seemed we had little choice.

I said, "Look, Mr. . . . dammit, what is your name, anyway?"

He hesitated. "James."

"Well, Mr. James, or I guess it should be Captain James—"

"It's my first name."

"What's the rest of it?"

A sigh. "James F. X. Corrigan."

"Francis Xavier?"

"None other. Fifty percent Irish on my Dad's side. County Cavan."

"Well, then, you ought to . . . oh." He wasn't looking at

me. "I get it," I said. "That's why you keep it a secret, huh? Corrigan. I bet you got tired of the jokes, didn't you? I bet an awful lot of clowns called you Wrong-Way Corrigan—"

"No relation at all," he said doggedly.

"Wrong-Way Corrigan," I said, as the waves of hysteria began to build. "What else? Wrong-way Corrigan. And . . . and we're heading for Ireland . . . and . . . oh, Christ, I bet we wind up in Los Angeles!"

19

But I was wrong. We didn't wind up in Los Angeles. The flight took ten hours instead of eight, and we very nearly did overfly Ireland, but at seven o'clock Irish time he bounced us down on the runway at Shannon Airport.

It was undoubtedly the worst flight in the history of aviation. We hit every air pocket and cross current between Montreal and Shannon, and we knew at once when each of our passengers shook off his drug-induced stupor. As soon as they straightened out, they promptly vomited. Everybody on the plane threw up at least once, and one poor woman had dry heaves for an hour running. Every last one of us was sick.

Everyone, that is, except Corrigan. Corrigan! There was no whiskey, but one of the captive guards had a pint of Cuban rum and the nurse's bag contained a bottle of grain alcohol, and between the two he kept himself fried all the way across the ocean. Corrigan! It wasn't enough that he flew the plane himself. He insisted on giving Seth and Randy a turn, and would have put Minna at the controls if

I'd let him.

Corrigan! He put us through a ten-hour wringer, and when the plane landed, we gave him a standing ovation. We sang a song to him—*C-O-Double R-I-, G-A-N Spells Corrigan, Corrigan.* We christened him Right-Way Corrigan and gifted him with quarts of Jameson Redbreast. We told each other that his name would live as long as birds held the monopoly on wings. We nominated him for Aviation's Hall of Fame—the Wright Brothers, Lindbergh, Earhart, and Right-Way Corrigan.

Never in the course of human events has any man earned so much acclaim for making so many people vomit.

During all of the backslapping and cheering, all the joyous excitement of being alive and on the ground and out of that hideous plane, through it all I tried to figure out what the Irish authorities would do with us. It would be no picnic, I was sure. Lengthy interrogation, some form of confinement, telegrams back and forth between Dublin Castle and Washington, Ottawa, Havana, and London.

I had forgotten what Ireland was like.

There was none of this. An official in a splendid green uniform took me aside and asked why we had made an unscheduled landing, and I explained very briefly what the Cubans had been doing and how we had dealt with the situation. He found the Cuban plot dastardly beyond belief, our action praiseworthy, Corrigan's performance heroic, Arlette a charming young lady, and Minna a treasure. He talked to a few of the others, confirmed my story, and filled out special visa forms for all of us so that we could stay around Ireland as long as we wanted. He may have filed a report, but I would guess it was something he never got around to.

And that's all.

Honestly.

Because no one made any noise. Ireland would have had to answer official inquiries from other nations, but there weren't any. Havana certainly didn't want to raise any static. They were out two guards, one pilot, one nurse, and one plane, and they could always hijack an airliner to even the score. They were hoping everyone would be very quiet about the whole thing.

Ottawa didn't know what had happened. They knew that they wanted to get their hands on Evan M. Tanner, American, and Arlette Sazerac, Canadian, but they didn't know we were in Ireland and would probably have rejoiced to learn we were out of Canada.

Washington probably didn't know anything, either. And wouldn't act unless forced to. And London was completely out of the picture. No one had the vaguest idea that there had been a plot to make Prince Philip a widower. As far as anyone knew, a batch of MNQ lunatics had made a successful attempt at dynamiting a fireworks barge. London cared as little about the affair as Modonoland.

I suppose you're wondering why the Cubans were collecting Negroes, and how they got Minna, and all that. So was I. I pieced out the story on the plane and someday I will probably have to explain it to the Chief. I'm afraid he'll think I'm putting him on.

Ready? They wanted to train American Negroes as revolutionaries to serve as shock troops in an eventual Black

Revolution. I suppose the riots generated enough wishful thinking to get the plan approved. Their theory was that heavy indoctrination under the influence of drug therapy could turn any Negro, whatever his prior political outlook, into a Castro-oriented terrorist.

I don't think they could have made it work, but who can tell? Pavlovian conditioning techniques have undergone considerable refinement of late, and so have drugs. Maybe they didn't even expect it to work but felt that it was worth a try for research purposes.

In any event, they were using the pavilion to kidnap Negroes. They would select someone, steer him over to the sliding panel, and throw the switch. When he landed, a guard downstairs slapped a wad of chloroform over his nose and that was that. They had put in the wrist brackets and such when they built the place, but they never even bothered to use them.

Then, using drugs, they interrogated their prisoners to see which fish were keepers and which ones they had to throw back. If a person had a family who would miss him, back he went. If his health was such as to make him useless to them, he too was returned to the world outside. Only a small proportion wound up permanently installed in the concrete block building. The rest were released within a day of their capture. Since they had been in a constant stupor, they had virtually no memory of what had gone on during the captive period, and probably lost the memory of the few hours preceding capture as well. Short-term amnesia, not much different from an alcoholic blackout, was certainly no great cause for alarm.

How did Minna get into the act? She was in the wrong

place at the wrong time, standing on the sliding panel just as a guard maneuvered a Negro onto it. This was by no means the first time this had happened. They caught quite a few Caucasians this way, kept them unconscious for a few hours, and released them unharmed. They would have done just this with Minna if the Royal Canadian Mounted Police hadn't contrived to make a front-page figure out of me. Once I had achieved total notoriety, they were in a quandary. Minna was now important, and if they released her and she turned up, a lot of people would be very intent on finding out where she had been. Then, too, the Cubans knew me as a member of several militant refugee organizations, and may have planned to use her to put pressure on me. Whatever they had in mind, they found it more expedient to keep her drugged than to let her go. Then, when Arlette sent them into a state of pure panic, they wanted to get her out of the country along with everyone else.

Thanks to Corrigan, they didn't make it.

And the Cubans wound up, all things considered, in almost as bad shape as they deserved. On our plane alone were sixty-seven American Negroes ranging in hue from blue-black to stratospheric-yellow, in age from eleven to forty-eight, and in politics from conservative pillars of the black bourgeoisie to the most rabid of black nationalists, and every last one of them was positive of one thing—that Cuba was no friend of theirs.

There were other planes that had not taken the famous Corrigan detour, other Negroes who had gone to Havana already. They didn't stay there long. Some of our passengers made phone calls to the States and some civil rights organizations sent discreet letters to the Cuban embassy requesting the immediate return of the abductees. There was no public uproar. The threat was enough, and back they all came, slipped quietly into Mexico and smuggled carefully across the Rio Grande.

What else? That covers half my list—*Minna* and *Assassination.* The other two items will have to wait awhile.

Heroin? It's still in that jacket. If I destroy it, the supply of heroin on the U.S. market will be stretched thin, and the price on the street will skyrocket, and the crime rate will soar, and a lot of poor junkies who have trouble enough already will be more uptight than ever.

Besides, the Union Corse knows how to hold a grudge. So it will have to go back to its wrongful owners. Still, it seems it ought to cost them a little. So when I get around to it, I'll send a note to a friend of mine on Corsica, and he'll set up a deal to sell the stuff back for a fraction of its value. Fraction or no, there should be enough money involved to make it interesting.

I'm in no hurry, though. Let 'em sweat a little.

Cops? I'm in even less of a hurry to clear that last point off the list. With the passage of time, Canadians and Americans alike should forget what an archcriminal I've been. I'll have Jerzy Pryzeshweski withdraw his kidnap nonsense, and that should clear the situation in the States. If the Chief pulls a string or two, Canada won't try to extradite me. They may never let me into the country. That's fine.

So here we all are, Arlette and Minna and I, very comfortably ensconced in a couple of rooms in Lord Edward Street, in Dublin. It is so deliciously cold here that we light a coal fire on the hearth every night. It rains every day, a light, clean, powdery rain. And the air is clean, and nobody is on strike, and there aren't any riots, and on one ever comes to the door, and we don't have a phone.

Arlette misses the tigerskin. It and the beret remain at her apartment, and it's doubtful whether we'll ever be able to recover them. Such skins, it seems, are extraordinarily expensive. Once we get the ransom money for the heroin, I'll see what I can do.

In the meantime, she has purchased a blonde wig. I haven't yet managed to turn up a Frankenstein mask, but we have hopes. Minna now speaks with the suggestion of a Dublin accent. She is learning Québecois French from Arlette and wants to learn to speak Irish, but so far we haven't run into anyone who knows how. She gets taken to the Dublin Zoo as often as she can manage it. Usually we get her to settle for a walk down to the River Liffey and a view of the gulls. I told her that if we stay here much longer, she will have to get a starched blue uniform and go to school every day. She didn't even have the courtesy to pretend I was serious.

We see Seth and Randy now and then. They drop in for meals. Most of their time is spent haunting the campuses at Trinity College and the National University, convinced that there must be some way to obtain marijuana in Ireland. If there is, they'll find it.

Corrigan flew home a week ago but as a passenger this time. The day he left, every Dublin newspaper covered the event and expressed the hope that he would return soon. I think he will; he enjoyed the city as much as it enjoyed him, which was considerably. The pubs hadn't been so lively since Behan died.

I guess we'll have to go back sooner or later. I must have a metric ton of mail at the Post Office by now. I'll have to find out whether Annalya has presented me with a brother or a sister for Todor, and what name it has been given. I'll also have to determine whether or not my friends in Africa have been eaten, and if so, by whom.

And I will have to report to the Chief.

I'd report to him right now, if I could. But that would contravene a key rule—I am never allowed to make contact with him. Nor could I if I wanted to. I don't know his name, or where he lives, or where he works, or much of anything about him.

And he can't get in touch with me, because he doesn't know where I am.

I hope nobody tells him.

Center Point Publishing
600 Brooks Road • PO Box 1
Thorndike ME 04986-0001 USA

(207) 568-3717

US & Canada:
1 800 929-9108

DW

99151